The Forever Experiment

A VALENTINE NOVELLA

SARAH A. BAILEY

This one is for the hyper-independent eldest daughters who've forgotten how to relax.

May you find yourself an acts of service golden retriever who lets you walk him like a dog in the streets, and makes you drop to your knees like a good little wife in the sheets.

Content Warnings

This book contains mature themes and is suitable for readers 18+.

Content includes: Explicit language, alcohol consumption, discussions of toxic relationships (past; off-page), brief workplace harassment and alluding to workplace sexual harassment, public sex and exhibitionism, oral sex, restraint and choking, and cum play.

Easton

Valentine's Day - 10 Years Ago

"SMACK YOUR GUM A little louder, pretty boy."

A smile teases my lips as the nickname echoes off the walls of the otherwise silent library. I lift my head from behind my laptop to find two almond-shaped, brown and gold flecked eyes looking back at me. They smolder with amusement despite her full lips screwed into a vexed frown.

"Not gum. Candy." I grin at her, holding up the box of Tart Hearts before I go back to chewing—louder this time.

She scoffs, gaze falling to her screen as she shakes her head. Her nails tap against the keys in a way that spells her annoyance. I know we're working on the same term paper for our Business Law 101 course. Most of our other classmates will procrastinate until Sunday night to get it done, opting to spend their Valentine's Day in more enticing ways, but I knew Maya would come down to the North Library to study tonight, and it's no surprise I ended up doing the same.

If I were going to ask anyone out on the most romantic of holidays, it'd be her.

She'd say no, though. So instead, I spend my evening actually getting ahead of my coursework for once while stealing glances at her from the table across the room, searching for the courage I know I won't find to speak to her.

I mean, I do speak to Maya often. We take many of the same courses, and that's not because I'm stalking her. We're both pre-law. Last term, we formed a study group with a few other students and we often meet up, though everyone else had plans tonight.

I met Maya last fall in an Introduction to Law and Literature course. She caught my eye the first day when she was the only student in the room with the gall to ask our professor for clarification on the syllabus, establishing herself as the most ambitious, outspoken, and driven woman I've ever met. And that's generous, considering my sister, Penelope, just got admitted to fucking Oxford.

I've lusted after her ever since, and sometimes, I swear I can see a matching passion in Maya's eyes, but whatever may be brewing beneath the surface, she sure as hell won't act upon it.

She's focused on school, her career, and her future one-hundred percent of the time. She's convinced men are nothing more than a waste of time, a deterrent to her success. Honestly, I can't say I disagree. I don't have much to offer besides an above-average cock and an eager tongue, but I'd be more than willing to slip her an orgasm or two between classes if it allowed me even a few moments alone with her.

There's something about Maya—her energy, her aura, her smile. It's the triumph I feel when I'm actually capable of pulling a laugh from that pretty mouth of hers. I'm addicted to her.

How do I go about telling her that, though?

Hey, I know you're way out of my league, but would you ever consider making me your personal boy toy because I'd rather be that to you than nothing at all?

I'm a fucking lunatic.

"If you want a piece, Maya baby, all you've got to do is walk those pretty legs over here and ask me nicely."

Those eyes lift to me over her screen, flaring with just a hint of allure. The first time she called me "pretty boy" was after I offered to take the lead witness freshman year on our university's Mock Trial team and she promptly told me to sit down before taking the lead herself. Which was to be expected, I'm not the most motivated student. I'm applying for law school because my dad is a doctor and my sister is going to discover lost cities someday, and I'm determined not to be the family fuck-up.

Regardless, the nickname stuck, just like I got stuck on her, and "Maya baby" followed not long after. She pretends to hate it, but the only thing she seemed to hate more was the three month period when I had stopped calling her that, because I thought she didn't like it.

She's complicated, but I'd spend a lifetime unraveling her nuances if I could.

"Shouldn't you be out getting yourself into trouble tonight?" Her voice is a purr, her movements like silk as she closes her laptop and stands from her chair. She strides toward me before planting her sweet, thick thighs on the edge of my table and holding out her palm.

I pull a heart out of the box, making sure I grab a blue one that reads "B Mine" before setting it in her hand and leaning back in my chair, crossing my arms behind my head. "Had better things to do."

"Like stalking me?" she asks, tossing the candy into her mouth without even looking at what it says.

"I do not stalk you," I scoff.

"Right. Of course you don't," she says, tossing her sleek, straight hair over her shoulder. "That's why you're at the North Library tonight when it's so much farther from your apartment than the Main Library on campus."

I raise my brow. "Now who's the stalker?"

She rolls her eyes, glancing away, though I catch the blush creeping up her cheeks.

It emboldens me. "Why aren't you out on a date tonight?"

"The only thing I'm dating is my coursework." She huffs a laugh. "Just like someday, I'll be married to my career." She shrugs. "I like it that way."

"We could always do that thing where if we reach forty and we're not married, we marry each other," I offer with a wink.

Her eyes flash to mine before she dips her head, hiding a smile. "And why would I want to marry you, pretty boy?"

I bite my lip, rocking in my chair, trying not to giggle like a child. Something about this interaction has me downright fucking giddy. "I'm great in bed."

"Mhmm." She lets out a disbelieving sigh, but her blush deepens.

"Please," I huff, feeling more confident than ever before. "Don't sit here and try to pretend you've never thought about it."

She bites her lip, refusing to look at me, though I watch her eyes track the flex in my arms where they're folded behind my head. It's the same way she watches my hands when I type, the movement of my tongue when I lick my lips because I've caught her staring. She's cataloging my body to imagine all the things I might be able to do with it.

I unfold my arms and run my palms down my thighs, and she watches that too.

"See? You're looking at my hands again."

Maya's eyes snap to mine, the gold in them blazing bright. "They're nice hands," she admits, nearly breathless.

"I can do a lot of nice things with them," I respond gruffly.

The air between us grows thick, the unspoken question hanging like a tether neither of us is sure the other wants to pull. I lean forward, looking up to where she still sits on the table in front of me. Slowly, I raise my hand and place it beside her thigh, lifting my pinky to make contact with her leg.

I pause there, allowing her time to move away, to tell me no. But she doesn't.

I circle my finger over the fabric of her tights. They're sheer, accented by a maroon-colored sweater dress and a pair of knee high boots I'd crawl to see her bare in.

"Easton," she breathes.

I immediately stop, but before I can pull my hand away, she's grasping the collar of my pullover and hauling me up to stand. I follow her lead, stepping between her legs and reveling at the way they spread for me.

One second of suspended time allows her eyes to meet mine, a year and a half of pent up tension and daydreams clashing in our gaze before she's pulling my shirt again, forcing my mouth to hers.

Her lips meet mine—a soft dichotomy to the fierceness with which she claims my mouth. Her hand curls around the nape of my neck, long nails twisting into my hair as she brushes her tongue across the seam of my lips possessively.

"Fuck, Maya," I groan, spurring her on as she grips me tighter, letting out a whimper of her own.

I slide my hands up her thighs, palms skating over the sheer tights and soft fabric of her sweater-dress until I'm grasping her hips. I tug her into me, our bodies flush, and I feel her gasp at my hard length now pressing into her. I drag my lips from hers, brushing along her jaw and down her neck, savoring the taste of her sweet flesh beneath my tongue.

She runs her fingers through my hair, thighs tightening around my waist. "I never do this."

"Thank God," I rasp against her skin.

I don't ever want to think about another man touching her hips or having his mouth on her flesh. I sink my teeth into her collarbone, desperate to be the only man doing that to her too.

"Rules," she says, causing me to pull back and look down at her. Her hair is ruffled, pupils blown wide, taking up her dark irises as she breathes heavily, staring at me with a lust-laced gaze.

"Rules?"

Maya nods. "This is a one-time thing, we're not going home together, and we never speak of it again."

"Even if I do a really, really good job?"

She huffs a laugh, shaking her head.

"Okay. We never speak of it again, unless..." I smirk. "We both cash in on that marriage pact when we're forty. Then, I'm going to bring up this night every chance I get until you let me repeat it over..." I bring my hand to her neck, gently closing my fingers around her throat. "And over..." I lean in, pressing my lips to her ear. "And over again."

"Easton," she breathes.

"Yeah, Maya baby?"

"Shut up and fuck me." She pulls back, bracing herself back against the table behind her as her legs spread wider. The sweater dress rides up her thighs, revealing smooth, dark skin.

My cock is raging against my jeans as I slide my palms up her flesh, dipping my fingers between her legs and grasping her sheer tights. "How important are these to you?"

"Not as important as feeling you touch me."

"Fuck." Our foreheads press together as we both glance down to where I fist the tights at the apex of her thighs. The rip of fabric mingles with our rapid breathing as I tear them open, granting me access to her bare skin.

I slip her dress higher so it bunches at her waist, looping my arms around her thighs as I fall to the floor in front of her, putting me at face-level with her pussy.

"What are you doing?" she hisses.

I brush a finger over the silk of her lace panties, slipping beneath the fabric and pulling it aside. She's already wet, glistening with arousal beneath the perfectly manicured triangle of dark hair. So *fucking hot*.

"Maya, baby, I've been craving your taste since we met." I lift my head, finding her flaming dark eyes searing through me. "You're not going to deny me that now, are you?"

"Shouldn't we..." She's breathless, chest heaving as she glances around the quiet library. "Try and be quick about this? We're technically in public."

She's nervous, clearly outside her comfort zone, and fuck if that doesn't spur me on, desperate to make sure this is the best sexual experience she'll ever have.

"My only priority is to feel you coming on my face, and if someone wants to interrupt that, they can fucking watch."

"Jesus Christ," she moans, head falling back.

"Is that a yes, Maya, baby?"

"God, Easton," she rasps, head snapping down to watch me move between her thighs. "Yes, please. Fuck."

She gasps as I tug her to the edge of the table, pressing on the inside of her knees to spread her wider. Her legs tremble as I pull her panties to the side once more before swiping my tongue up her slit.

I flick her clit in a teasing lick before moving down to her center and thrusting inside her and dragging my mouth back. I feel her nails in my hair, pulling at my strands and forcing my face exactly where she wants me.

I suck her bud into my mouth, swirling my tongue around it as I nip with my teeth, teasing a finger at her center. She whimpers when I enter her, bending my finger at the knuckle to make a beckoning motion, massaging her in just the right spot.

"Christ, Maya. You taste so fucking good, baby."

My cock throbs as I continue to lap at her, desperate to get inside her wet warmth. Her hold on my hair tightens as her thighs tremble around my head. Her moans—quiet and soft at first—start to grow louder. She's losing control, no longer concerned with fear that we may be caught like this.

She bucks her hips against my face, chasing friction and ecstasy, desperate for the release I'm about to give her. I slip a second finger inside her, curling both and moving my hand faster while I match the rhythm with my tongue on her clit.

"Easton," she breathes, and I damn near come at the breathless moan of my name from her lips. I press my free hand against my cock, adding pressure to quell the release begging to barrel through me. I *need* to be inside her.

Her quivering legs crush my face as her hand behind my head presses me to her center so hard, I think I might suffocate, but fuck, I am not complaining.

"Atta girl. Let me taste you."

"Fuck," she gasps, and I feel her climax rush through her, drenching my fingers. She lets go of my head, body trembling, as she falls back onto the desk.

I let her ride it out as her hips continue to move against my face, leaving her clit and slipping my tongue inside her, allowing her release to coat my mouth as I savor her taste.

"Easton, my god," she continues as she floats back down to Earth.

I don't stop until I've wrung every last drop of pleasure from her, sitting back on my knees to take in her glowing dark skin, trembling limbs, and wild hair as she lays back on the table, satisfied by *me*.

She slowly raises back up to sit, and I get to my feet, towering above her. She lifts her gaze, eyes hooded and lust-laced as a soft, sated smile tugs at her full lips. "Are you gonna fuck me now, pretty boy?" I reach into my back pocket for my wallet, pulling out the condom I keep inside it. Maya's eyes blow wide as I flip the foil in my fingers. "Damn. You come prepared."

"When you're around? Always, Maya baby. Never know when a miracle might present itself."

"Fucking me is a miracle?" she muses.

"I haven't fucked you yet, but baby, eating that pretty cunt of yours sure felt like a dream come true."

I tear the wrapper open with my teeth as I pop the button on my jeans. She watches with rapt attention, eyes flaring and bottom lip slipping beneath her teeth as I pull out my cock. Her gaze rapidly darts between my face and where I fist myself. Satisfaction rushes through me at the sight of her salivating for me.

I roll the condom over my tip and down my length before guiding it between her legs. "Lean back on your elbows. I want you to watch me sink inside this perfect pussy."

"Easton," she moans. "Your fucking mouth."

"Are you referring to the way it felt against your clit or the words coming out of it?"

"Both," she whimpers as I swipe my head through her wet slit, notching at her center.

Her breath hitches, and a groan falls from my throat as I push inside her fully, feeling her wrap around my cock in a vise grip. "Fuck, Maya, you're so goddamn tight."

My mind reels at the sight of me lost between her perfect thighs, knowing I'm inside her flawless body. I feel her inhale swiftly, her hands grasping my biceps, nails digging into my skin as her hips begin to jerk forward.

"I need you to move," she whispers. "I need you to fuck me. Now."

"Wrap your legs around my waist," I growl.

She complies, and I retreat, watching the way my cock is soaked in her arousal before I slam back into her hard enough to shake the table beneath us. I grip her hips, driving into her as she meets me thrust for thrust.

One of her hands wraps around the nap of my neck, pulling our heads together as her mouth crashes against mine. I moan at the soft feel of her lips paired with the urgent way she moves them against mine, darting her tongue into my mouth, knowing she can taste herself.

Every atom in my body is hyperactive, addicted to each inch of skin I'm able to feel. Her calf brushes against my ribs and her fingers twine in my hair, her breath against my tongue and her soft flesh beneath my hands. Her pussy tightens around my cock, my entire body blazing at the feel of it.

She's electric, and being inside her feels like a fucking dream.

White hot pleasure zips through my nerves, settling in the base of my spine as my body pulses with need. My heart wracks against my chest as her moans grow louder, reaching a crescendo that tells me she's fucking close.

"Maya, baby, come on my cock," I whimper into her mouth. "Please. Make a mess all over me. I need it so bad."

Her breath catches as she thrashes, both arms falling over my shoulders and nails digging into my back as her legs tense around my hips. "Easton," she cries, breath hot against my neck.

I feel her tighten, igniting my release as that pleasure in the base of my spine explodes. My arm bands around her waist, forcing us as close as possible as my other arm finds the base of her neck and fists her hair.

I'm vaguely aware of the way I groan her name as I spill inside her, muffling my sounds against her shoulder. My mind blanks, and stars explode behind my eyes, my entire being focused on where our bodies connect, on the feel of her mouth against my skin, her hands in my hair, my cock pulsing inside her as she spasms around me.

I don't know how long we lay like that before either of us finds the strength to pull back, but I keep my hands on her skin, prolonging every second I get to touch and feel her. My lips drag against her jaw, finding her mouth.

Her eyes are hazed, swimming in passion as she looks at my lips, running her hands up and down my back, legs still locked at my waist. "That was..." she pants through staccato breath. "Wow."

"I told you I'm good in bed." I smile against her mouth.

"You're good on table. You might still be terrible in bed."

A laugh bursts out of me, and I realize this being a one-time-thing might actually fucking kill me. I am downright obsessed with this woman. "You wanna find out?"

She pulls back, tilting her head. Her features soften at my question, and I want to kiss the flush from her cheeks and the sweat from her temple, laying claim to the reaction my body has had on hers.

"I told you it would only happen once, Easton," she whispers.

I tuck her hair behind her ear. "Can you blame a guy for trying?"

She bites her lip, hiding a smile as she shakes her head. A small whimper escapes her mouth as I pull out of her and dispose of the condom, hiding it in my empty coffee cup and tossing it in the trash beside our table. I tuck myself back into my jeans as she slips off her ruined tights and tosses them into the trash too. I grab her hips once more, lifting her off the table to help straighten out her dress as she combs fingers through her hair.

"Can I walk you home?" I ask.

"I suppose. If you insist," she teases as we clear our tables and grab our bags.

I place my hand on the small of her back, guiding her through the main doors of the library, holding one open for her as we step outside into the frigid February evening.

"Fuck, I didn't think about how cold it is when I ruined those tights," I say as she shivers beside me.

"It's okay. It's a short walk." Her teeth chatter with every word.

I slip off my coat, tossing it around her shoulders. I don't know how much it's going to help with her bare legs exposed to the elements, but it's all I have to offer.

It's quiet as we make our way to her apartment near campus, but it's not the awkward I-just-fucked-a-class-mate-in-the-library silence you'd expect. It's a comfortable I-just-came-so-hard silence that makes you want to crawl in bed with the person you were intimate with and hold them all night.

As we reach Maya's complex, she rifles through her purse for her keys before facing me and shrugging off my coat. "Thanks for letting me wear your jacket," she says softly. "And for...um...the orgasm."

"Orgasms." I smile. "Plural."

She huffs, rolling her eyes. "Right. Thank you for the *multiple* orgasms, Easton."

She's so fucking pretty when she's rolling her eyes at me. I can't stop myself from blurting, "Can I kiss you goodnight?"

Her lips tilt up soft, tone gentle as she says, "We're not doing this again. It's not going to become a thing." Her eyes drop to the ground. "I'm not going to get wrapped up in a relationship when I'll be moving for law school in just a few months."

"I understand." I cup her face, forcing her to look at me. "So, if I only get to have you once, can I at least do it right?"

She softens at that, her smile growing wider as she nods. I bring my other hand to her cheek now, twisting my fingers in her hair as I drag her mouth to mine. I feather my lips between hers, kissing her softly and tasting her gently, desperate to prolong the moment as long as possible.

Something about Maya just feels right when she's pressed against my chest, mouth on mine. I know we're nothing, that we'll never be anything, but fuck, I wish that wasn't the case. The way she moans as our tongues dance makes me wonder if she's thinking the same, and it's cemented when she fists my sweater and hauls us closer together, like she's not ready for it to end either.

She pulls away first—because I sure as fuck am not going to—blinking rapidly, like she's floating back to reality, waking up from a dream. I feel the same, swiping my thumb against her cheek one final time before forcing myself to step away.

She stumbles toward the door of her apartment, and because I'm a glutton for punishment, I can't stop myself from calling out as she slides her key into the lock. "Don't forget about that marriage pact, Maya baby. I'll be calling you at midnight on your fortieth birthday, and I expect an answer."

"Goodnight, Easton," she tsks with a laugh.

"Happy Valentine's Day!" I shout as she opens her door.

She stands in the frame, winking at me before shutting it behind her.

1

Easton

"DERRICK, I PROMISE, I do not need your cut-out paper hearts strung above my door."

"Of course, you do. They're for good luck so you can get laid on next week's holy day."

"Those hearts aren't going to do anymore for my sex life than they are for yours," I mutter to my assistant, watching him stand on a chair in the doorway to my office as he strings pink, red, and white heart-shaped garland above the frame.

He spent the better part of the morning drawing and cutting them out at his desk outside my office, and I'm suddenly feeling the need to put out an ad for a new assistant.

"At least I have a sex life," he sings.

I scoff, flipping him my middle finger before going back to my computer screen. Winter in Boise is normally a busy time for personal injury litigation. Slick roads, crashed cars, you know the drill—though my firm has been unseasonably slow since the holidays.

My sex life is no different.

It's only February 10th, I remind myself. I've been irrationally afraid I'm going to find myself having a dry year, and Derrick's antics don't fucking help.

Thank God I've got a trip planned to see my sisters at the end of the month. I need to get out of this office and out of the cold.

"Did you eat grapes and sit beneath a table on New Year's Eve?" he asks as he steps off the chair and begins to pick up his scraps of paper.

"No, I didn't fucking eat grapes..." My words die on my tongue as my eyes snag on a newsletter from the American Bar Association.

Normally, those newsletters go straight into the trash folder, but the subject line of this one has me opening it immediately: *ABA Winter Conference Keynote Speaker is Maya Atler.*

Maya. Fucking. Atler.

The name rings through my head like a familiar wind, like the way it feels when I visit my parents back in Oregon and step out of my car, feeling the sea breeze on my face after too many months away. Though with Maya... It has been years.

She gave me one incredible night before swearing never again. We still met up in study group, but she ensured she kept a healthy distance, like she couldn't trust herself around me, and as satisfying as it was to know, it still fucking stung.

By the time she was accepted to Harvard Law at the end of that year, we were nothing more than classmates again. I've checked in every so often throughout the years online, admiring her success from afar, but when I stumbled upon a Facebook update showcasing her engagement, I decided to quit her cold turkey. It didn't matter that seven years had passed—I was still stuck on her.

I've dated on and off throughout the years, even attended the wedding of one of my exes, but for some reason, that didn't burn nearly as bad as finding out Maya was going to marry another man.

I guess after two years of crushing on her and one night of having her, I figured that if she had wanted to be with someone, she'd have been with me. My efforts weren't futile, and the allure wasn't made up in my head. She had wanted me too—she just wanted a career more. That, I could understand. I wasn't the problem. No, love itself had been the problem—the distraction she didn't need—and that was something I could live with.

Finding out it was just me who wasn't good enough after all—that hurt.

Still, I can't stop myself from passively scrolling through the newsletter, stopping on the paragraph written about her and her accomplishment of being one of the youngest attorneys in the country to establish a firm, having a staff underneath her and an office in a fancy high rise in San Diego. I also can't stop myself from noticing her last name remains Atler, and I hope the ring-absent photo of her in the newsletter is recent, because that would mean she may not be engaged after all. At least, not anymore.

She's beautiful as ever, dressed impeccably in what is no doubt a designer suit, bright, wide-set smile on display. Her deep brown eyes are dark and glittering, her hair braided, whereas it had been straight the last time I'd seen her. Her lips are full, glittering with pink lip gloss that makes me reminisce about the way they tasted.

I'm so curious about her, how she ended up in San Diego when I knew she was originally from Chicago, attending college in Boise, law school in Boston. I'm not aware of any ties she has to California, though I wouldn't blame her for moving down for the weather alone. I want to know if she feels as accomplished as she set out to be, or if there is a new, larger dream she's working toward now. I want to ask what happened to her fiancé and if she's single now. Most of all, I want to ask her if she ever thinks of me.

That last realization has me abruptly standing from my desk and striding out of my office, much to the confusion of my assistant, who was definitely in the middle of a sentence I wasn't listening to.

I head down the hall toward my boss' office: Harvey Lewis. I rasp my knuckles on the door, waiting for permission to enter before I twist the knob and crack it open. "You busy?"

"If I was, I wouldn't have let you come in," he says, clicking away at his computer screen before rolling back from his desk and looking at me.

"I won't take up much time. I just wanted to ask if anyone from the firm is attending the ABA conference this year?"

Harvey shakes his head. "Not this year. I normally try to go, but with it being on Valentine's Day? My wife would have my head."

Shit. It's on Valentine's Day?

I hadn't paid any attention to the dates when I was reading through that newsletter.

"How would you feel about me attending?"

He raises a brow at me. "I'd feel like you were looking for an excuse to fuck around in Vegas for two days, and I'm not about to have this firm looking like an embarrassment."

I frown, though I suppose I kind of deserve it. I'm not known for being the most motivated individual. I am known, however, for being a complete fuck off.

"Honestly, I didn't even realize it was happening in Vegas," I say truthfully. "I just noticed that my undergrad study partner is the keynote speaker, and I'd love a chance to go support her. Plus..." I draw, quickly pulling out my phone and re-opening the email. "I was really intrigued by the..." My thumb flies across my screen as I attempt to scan the newsletter while maintaining eye contact with my boss. "Corporate Sustainability workshop."

"Right," Harvey murmurs, turning back to his computer. I watch light flash across his eyes as he searches for something before raising them to me. "You're telling me you were buddies with Maya Atler?"

"Oh, have you met her?"

He chuckles. "No, but I've heard of her. She's impressive."

"Incredibly."

"What the hell was she doing hanging around you?"

I force a smile. "You know what? Why don't I ask her at the conference?"

Harvey lets out a belly-deep laugh, leaning back in his chair again. "I don't mind if you go, Easton, but I need you to actually try and get some benefit out of it, okay? Go to that damn sustainability...thing. Just don't embarrass me."

I lift my hand in a mock salute. "No problem, sir."

"Get the fuck out of my office, Easton," he grumbles, turning back to his desk.

"Right away, sir." I click my heel, a stupid, dopey ass smile on my face.

2

Maya

Fuck. Fuck. Fuckity-fuck.

I pace behind the curtain, nausea rolling through me as I frantically read over my notecards, mentally preparing myself for the talk I'm about to give on...well, me. My upbringing, my career, my journey to becoming one of the youngest founders of a Black woman-owned literary law firm in the country.

I'm honored, and no doubt deserving, considering the work I've put into getting here, but *goddammit*, I hate public speaking.

"Miss Atler?" one of the event assistants asks. "Five minutes until you're introduced."

I nod, continuing to pace.

"Oh, and someone left a gift for you back here. It's on your chair."

That has me pausing. I scurry over to the small dressing area they had set up backstage, my heels clicking against the floor impatiently. Sure enough, sitting on my chair is a bouquet of mixed pink and red flowers, stems wrapped in a pink ribbon.

A box of Tart Hearts sits beside the flowers, the holiday candy we shared last time we were together. Lastly, a pink card is tucked into the petals of the flowers. I step up to them, slipping it out and opening it.

Roses are red,
Violets are blue,
~~This Valentine's Day~~
~~I want to be with you~~

Break a leg, Maya baby
– pretty boy

Clearly, it was a pre-printed card picked up from a grocery store, with the last line crossed out, his message hand-written and signed at the bottom.

Easton Mason.

A name I haven't thought or heard in such a long time, but a pleasant one, nonetheless. It has been a long, *long* time; I can count the number of conversations we've had on one hand since the night he was inside me.

I blew him off after we had sex in the library that night, because although it—to this day—is arguably the best sex I've ever had, and taking that risk with him is the most alive I'd felt in years, as soon as it was over, I knew I was at a high risk of falling too far in with him. I quite literally couldn't afford the distraction—my scholarships and my law school acceptance relied on total focus.

I kept him at arm's-length after that and have avoided thinking about him ever since. I've always been a little afraid I hurt him. I think Easton felt the same way about me that I did about him, except he was all in—ready to take the risk. I knew that before I had sex with him, and I did it anyway because I was desperate to feel something, not expecting Easton Mason to make me feel *everything*.

Including guilt for pushing him away afterward because a relationship at that time would've been detrimental to my future.

In the back of my mind, I've always kind of assumed he hates me now, but familiar nicknames, the candy from that night, and the flowers wishing me luck have a smile tugging at my lips, my nerves momentarily forgotten.

Is he here?

I know from mutual college friends that he attended law school at the University of Oregon before returning to Boise to work for the same firm he interned with during our junior year.

I've attended the American Bar Association conference every year since I founded Atler and Associates, and I've never heard of Easton Mason being in attendance.

"Miss Atler," the event assistant says, breaking my thoughts. "We're ready for you."

That moment of peace vanishes, sharpness shooting through my stomach, sending my heart in a chaotic rhythm as it thrashes against my chest. My vision feels tunneled, my legs trembling as I turn around, forcing a smile at the girl. "Alright."

I take a deep breath before following her to the curtain. She peeks her head behind the stage as we listen to a mentor and former professor of mine introduce me to the crowd before applause begins. She exits the other end of the stage, and suddenly, the curtain is being ripped aside, exposing me to blinding lights and loud crowds.

I take one more breath, hearing my heels click upon the floor as I walk out to the center and turn to face the audience head-on. My stomach is in my throat, and I suddenly regret that I didn't pee before coming out here. My hands are shaking as I grip the edge of the podium, breath short and fast when I lean into the mic. I know that the moment I use my voice, it's going to be trembling, giving away my fear to everyone in the room.

The audience politely claps as I allow myself to countdown from three before I jump in and begin speaking, no matter how bad I'll sound. It's when a deafening whistle echoes through the auditorium that my eyes snap from my shaking hands to the crowd in front of me.

All I can make out are silhouettes blocked by the stage lights, but as I scan the seats, I'm caught on one figure sitting three rows back on the far end.

Easton Mason is standing, slowly pulling two fingers from his mouth, flashing me that megawatt smile I always adored. He raises his hand, giving me a small wave.

I know the cheesiest grin is stretching my face, and suddenly, it's not nerves providing the swirling sensation inside my body, but the familiar flap of butterfly wings.

I begin to speak, and my voice is steady and strong. My eyes stay on him the entire time.

3

Easton

"EXCUSE ME, DO YOU know where I can find Miss—" My words stop short when I spot her turning the corner outside the auditorium, a gaggle of adoring attorneys at her sides, complimenting her speech and her phenomenal career. I smile at the event worker. "Never mind."

Leaning against the wall with my arms crossed, I watch her as she stops, deep in conversation with the group of people around her, positively glowing as she shakes their hands and expresses her gratitude for their many, many compliments. Sun filters through the paneled windows behind her, backlighting her like a goddamn halo.

When an admirer of hers moves to walk away, her eyes snag on mine as she follows their movements. She has been smiling, but I don't miss the way her grin widens and her eyes somehow seem to shine brighter when she's looking at me.

She remains composed while she finishes her conversations, but her eyes can't seem to stop catching mine every few seconds. Even from across the hallway, I notice the blush accenting her cheeks, her gaze dropping when I catch her looking at me—which is every time, because my eyes unabashedly do not leave her—secretive smiles playing at her lips.

I've never shied away from pursuing a woman I'm interested in, and often, that interest is returned. I'm no stranger to hidden glances, flushed faces, or batting lashes. Though, there is something about the way it feels to see Maya having that reaction at nothing more than my eyes on her. It's powerful, whatever humming current flows between us. It's like a lasso wrapped around my chest, tugging me toward her inch by inch. I can only recall feeling this kind of power once before in my life—the last time Maya Atler was in it.

She shuffles the bouquet of flowers I bought her from one arm to the other as she shakes the hands of the last few people standing around her. As they dissipate, she turns to me, a wide smile wrecking her normally cool, collected composure. "Hi, pretty boy."

My arms open on instinct, and as if her excitement gets the best of her, she barrels toward me, crashing into them. I lock mine around her waist, lifting her in the air and spinning her around. "Hi, Maya baby."

She lets out a sigh against my shoulder, taking a step out of my arms as I set her down. I kind of wish she'd stay. She flips her long braids over her shoulder, giving me a once over.

"You look good." She nods, as if agreeing with her own assessment.

"I'd say the same, but *good* isn't the right word for how you look. You're a fucking masterpiece."

"Easton." She laughs under her breath. "I can't believe you're here. It's so nice to see you."

It's more than nice to see her. It's like a damn dream come true.

"You too." I nod down the hallway. "Walk with me?"

"Sure." She smiles. As we make our way toward the front of the hotel, she loops an arm through mine. "I mean, what're the odds?"

"Pretty high," I laugh, "considering I came here for you."

She stops, turning to face me, brows deep set over her shimmering brown eyes. "You came *just* to see me?"

I nod.

"Why?"

I shrug, attempting to remain nonchalant. "I saw you featured in the newsletter, and my boss wasn't able to make the conference this year, so I came in his place. I wanted to see you speak and be here to support."

Her face softens. "That's so sweet."

I shrug again, but I fail at hiding my triumphant smile.

"But, you know, the conference has a lot of incredible workshops and other speakers. There is a ton to learn."

"You're the best benefit, and I learned a lot from you today."

She huffs, shaking her head with a playful roll of her eyes. "So, are you here alone, or?"

"That your way of asking if I'm single?" I ask as we step onto an escalator to the lobby of the hotel.

"No." She leans back against it, facing me. "I figure you could've come with a colleague or an assistant."

"Nope. In fact, this is very much a retreat from my assistant." My lips tug upward. "He likes to play match-maker, because, you know...I'm single. Since you were curious."

She hums contemplatively but doesn't respond. We step off the escalator, and Maya begins strutting toward the elevators at the far end of the lobby that lead to one of the two towers of the hotel. "Well, I have a dinner I'm supposed to attend in a few hours, so I'm going to go freshen up and—"

"Bail on dinner and get a drink with me instead." My tone comes out far more desperate than I intended, but the sight of her walking away from me again is activating my fight or flight, and I guess I feel like fighting.

Maya pauses in front of me, her long braids swaying as she spins on a high, black heel and faces me. The pencil skirt she has on hugs her hips flawlessly, and as we've been walking, I've noticed the way it's rode up her panty-hose clad thighs, making me wonder if those are as easy to rip through as that pair of tights was all those years ago.

My eyes drag up her body, because prior to this mo-ment, I hadn't allowed myself a decent look.

When I reach her face, her gaze is glued to me, offering a cool assessment. "You know, you didn't even ask if I'm single." She scrunches her nose. "Maybe the dinner plans I have tonight are with my boyfriend."

I shake my head. "First of all, the dinner you're referring to is hosted by the Bar Association and is for all speakers and workshop leaders. I looked it up." I step toward her. "I also know it's not a requirement to attend."

"It's a networking opportunity."

"And," I interrupt her, because I wasn't finished speaking, "if you were dating someone who was not front row in that fucking auditorium, hanging onto every word you say, waiting for you afterward to show the entire goddamn planet—and, most importantly, you—how proud and amazed and in awe of you they are, then they do not deserve to sit across from you at a dinner table." Suddenly, I'm close enough to watch her eyes go molten, to track the way her throat moves as she swallows, the expansion of her lungs as her breathing elevates. "So for that reason, I really fucking hope you're single, Maya."

She licks her lips, eyes fluttering to the floor. "I'm single."

"Good." I pass her, continuing toward the elevator. My room is in the same wing of the hotel, so regardless, we're heading in the same direction.

"But," she continues, catching up to me, "the dinner is a networking opportunity I can't miss."

I stop in front of the elevator doors, pressing the up arrow. "That you can't miss, or that you don't want to?" I glance down at her. "When's the last time you took a night off?"

She opens her mouth as if she's about to argue, but as I watch her eyes search her memory, her lips clamp shut.

Sure enough, she's failing to remember the last time she gave herself a break.

I'm smiling triumphantly as the elevator chimes and the doors slide open. I place my hand on the small of her back as I guide her inside, relishing the feel of my skin against her body.

Once we're both in, I press the button for floor eleven, where my room is. Maya presses the button for floor thirty. My eyes flash to hers, catching a smirk. "I may not know how to take a day off, pretty boy, but I can afford a suite."

I huff a laugh, scratching at the scruff along my jaw.

"You wanna show me what it looks like?" I ask, biting my lip to hide my grin.

The elevator comes to a stop at my floor.

"Didn't I tell you that was a one-time-thing?" she asks, though the tone in her voice has dropped, flowing from her lips like soft, seductive velvet.

"Can you blame a guy for trying?" I wink as I step out of the elevator. "I'll be down in the lobby at seven tonight to take you out in case you decide you'd like to cash in on that night off." Spinning around before the doors can close, I add, "And remember, Maya baby: burn out leads to failure."

She's biting the inside of her cheek to keep from laughing as the elevator doors close.

4

Maya

"I GUESS I'M NOT attending that dinner tonight," I mutter to myself, adjusting my black denim jacket for the umpteenth time as I stare at myself in the mirror.

I had planned to wear a satin blouse tucked into black trousers and my favorite pair of Dolce & Gabbana pumps for the speaker's dinner tonight. Somehow, I ended up in a deep pink lace bodysuit that outlines my breasts a little too perfectly and flaunts far too much cleavage for it to be acceptable to wear to a business dinner, especially paired with the black faux leather skirt that hugs every inch of skin I have to offer and rests at my mid-thigh. My lips are nearly as pink as my top, glossy and accented by a cat eye. I tossed my braids into a high pony, letting two long strands frame my face. The oversized, black denim jacket is the only modest thing about me right now, down to the fuchsia Valentino platforms that scream *fuck me*.

I tell myself I chose these shoes because they not only match the body suit and platforms are easier to walk in, but let's honest—that's not the only reason. I'm definitely dressed for a date. I said I wasn't sure if I'd bail on the dinner to go out with Easton, but then, I came back to my room, showered, and ended up standing in front of the mirror dressed like this, so I guess my auto-pilot chose for me.

Though, this *isn't* a date. Definitely not.

Just two old college friends catching up.

College friends who once had sex. The best sex I've ever had, even a decade later.

But I'm not thinking about that.

Liar! The designer fuck-me heels adorning my feet seem to scream.

I tug at the hem of my skirt and turn around to check my back side, straightening out my jacket before finally murmuring, "Fuck it" and grabbing my purse from the side table. I brought this outfit as a backup, a *just in case* I decided to actually go out on the strip while I'm in Vegas. I assumed I wouldn't—I never do. I don't go out with friends at home in San Diego, not when I visit my family in Chicago, and never when traveling for work. I either don't have the time, the energy, or the self-confidence for it.

Tonight, it's self-confidence that's eating away at me.

Especially knowing I'm about to go out with Easton, of all people. The last time he saw me, I was twenty-two and had a metabolism that can only be described as mythical. Now, even though I take two yoga classes a week and attempt to consume a full serving of vegetables every day, my body looks different than it did back then.

Sure, Easton looked like he was choking on his tongue when he saw me for the first time today, and he may have referred to me as a fucking masterpiece, but he could've just been trying to be nice. Gas me up after my big speech. Who knows.

Before I can talk myself out of the night entirely, I swipe my room key and head out the door.

I find Easton standing at a bar near the front entrance of the casino in the same outfit he had worn to the conference earlier. Suddenly, I wonder how high maintenance I look for having changed when I catch Easton lifting his head, blinking as he rears back. His jaw drops as his easy blue eyes blow wide, and my mind begins to scream that I'm definitely wearing the wrong thing.

He clutches his chest, and that dropped jaw morphs to a wide grin as he mouths: *bombshell.*

The twister of nerves wreaking havoc on my stomach fades to nothing at his laugh. It's the same feeling I had when I was giving a speech earlier; every time I got afraid or insecure, I'd look at him and feel settled. As I reach him, he lets out a low whistle, extending his arm toward me.

I take it, saying, "One drink. I've got to get a good night's rest because I'm attending several workshops to-morr—"

"Goddamn," he rasps. "You look un-fucking-real, Maya. Makin' me the luckiest man in Vegas tonight." He spins me around, giving himself a full view of my outfit.

"I feel overdressed. You didn't even change."

He laughs. "Because I brought exactly two outfits. Plus," he drops my arm before gesturing to himself, "I still look damn good. Not that it matters. Nobody is going to be looking at me when I'm standing next to you."

My ex, Anthony, used to say the same thing, except it was always laced with venom.

I'm invisible when it comes to you.

I'd met him at Harvard, moved to San Diego for him too. His father was a renowned immigration attorney there, and Anthony was dead set on taking over the firm when he finished college. They have a legacy in the area—highly respected and well known. While the family and the firm's praise is more than deserved, Anthony took issue when I decided to open my own practice.

When I made a name for myself, when I was featured in articles and invited to seminars, he took personal offense. Even though we operated in completely different branches of law, he saw us as competitors, and he couldn't handle being with a woman who was more successful. He wanted to be the guest of honor at all times, never the plus-one.

I refused to diminish my achievements to make space for his spotlight, and in the end, we deteriorated. He also hated when I dressed provocatively, complained about the way I chew my food, and was flabbergasted when I told him that while I'd love to have children someday, I have every intention of being a working mother.

I should've known long before I finally called it quits that we weren't the right fit, but after watching everyone around me fall in love, get married, and find that seemingly impossible balance of work and life, I was desperate for it too.

"Is that a problem for you?" I ask.

Easton blinks. "Is what a problem for me?"

"If my outfit causes people to look in my direction more often than they look in yours?"

He chuckles, rubbing a broad, strong hand across his jaw. "Not even a little. It's an honor to have you on my arm, Maya, baby." He holds it out to me, and I smile as I loop mine around his elbow.

Again, that settling sensation erupts inside my belly, spreading through my chest, allowing me to breathe easier than I have all day. I packed this outfit because the most confident version of myself, the one I feel I lost so many years ago, would love it. I packed this outfit on the slight hope I might locate that lost confidence and gain the strength to wear it, though I felt so sure I wouldn't.

Somehow, I'm certain it's Easton Mason's words, his smile and sultry eyes—the way he strides through the casino like I'm a priceless piece of art he's honored to carry—giving me that conviction I need, believing I'm every bit the fucking masterpiece he says I am.

We step out into the cool February air, the lights of the strip blinding bright, the sounds of Sin City echoing around us. I turn to Easton, multitudes of color cascading across his handsome face. "So, did you have a place in mind?"

He smiles mischievously. "Yep."

Without another word, he takes my hand, dragging me behind him. We turn right, heading toward The Flamingo, and onto an escalator that'll take us on a bridge to cross over Las Vegas Boulevard. We stop momentarily at the top of it, looking out at the lights in front of us.

Paris towers above on one side, the bright blue balloon reflecting over the Bellagio fountains. This time of February isn't crawling with tourists the way the spring and summer are, and while I'd never describe Vegas as romantic, it feels...nice next to Easton. He waits patiently as I admire the skyline, and when I'm finished, we continue in the direction of Cesar's Palace.

"Where are we going?" I ask.

"You'll see."

We exit the escalator, and Easton takes us to what appears to be a giant, white circus tent. He walks right up to it, and I realize it's some kind of outdoor bar. Tapping his fingers against the counter, he smiles at me, only slightly taller when I'm in heels. "What flavor do you want?"

"Flavor?" I ask.

He nods behind the bar, and I realize the massive slushie machines in front of us. "Cherry, pina colada, or lime?"

A giggle bursts out of me. "This is what you had in mind when you asked to take me out for a drink?"

"Well, what did *you* have in mind?"

I snort. "I don't know. Cosmos at the Cosmopolitan?"

"Please," he tsks. "That's lawyer Easton and Maya nonsense. We don't need to be lawyers all the time." A strand of chestnut-colored hair falls over his forehead as he drops an elbow on the bar and turns toward me. "Look, you told me you'd have one drink, so I'm getting you *one* drink." He nods toward a couple beside us as they're handed a two-foot-tall plastic cup with a lid and a curly straw. "What flavor?"

I bite my lip, contemplating whether I throw caution to the wind and put my life in the hands of Easton Mason for the evening. "Fuck it." I sigh. "I want a mix of all three."

"Atta girl." He winks, and my insides go molten at his tone.

"Just one, and then I'm going back to the hotel, okay?"

He straightens his face, offering a mock salute before pulling out his wallet and tossing his card on the counter, ordering us each our own ridiculous slushie from the bartender.

"I'll agree to that, but I have a condition of my own." He crosses his arms, leaning a hip against the bar. "While you're drinking your *one* drink, I'm going to take you to my favorite place on the Strip."

"Where's that?"

"The promenade at the Linq. It's a lot calmer than other areas, mostly shops and restaurants. Outdoor and sparkling with lights. You'll like it, I think." That does sound nice. I've never been into the bar or club scene, which was part of the reason I didn't have plans to go out much on this trip. "Then, I'm going to take you on the High Roller."

"Oh, fuck no." I shake my head. "I don't do big ass wheels."

He laughs in a way that reminds me of the salt breeze brushing against my cheeks on a rare day spent at the beach back home. "You can't do Vegas in one night, and I don't know when or if you'll return. Even if you do, you may not be with me, so I already know you won't have as much fun. I want to make sure you see as much of the city as you can in the time you have, and the easiest way to do so is up in the air."

Damn him for making sense.

There are a few people I've connected with at the conference who mentioned going to a club or gambling in one of the casinos, and I've always had a hard time in those situations. I get claustrophobic easily, so crowded spaces with low lighting, loud noises, and lack of personal space don't bode well for me. I remember casually mentioning this to Easton once in college when he asked why I didn't attend many parties, but I never thought it was something he'd remember.

"Are you amenable to my terms?" He smiles slyly.

"Fine. I'll do your big wheel and drink this insane slushie, and then I'm going to bed."

"Say you accept the terms, Maya, baby. This is a work trip, after all."

I roll my eyes. "I accept the terms, pretty boy."

He holds his hand out to me, and I place my palm in his. Instead of shaking it, he brings it to his mouth, brushing his lips along my knuckles. Sparks alight along my skin, starting in the place his mouth meets my flesh and spreading like wildfire through my body, embers blazing in my core.

"Hand kisses are legally binding, by the way," he says as he gently drops my arm and grabs our drinks from the bar, handing mine to me.

"Shit," I respond, suddenly breathless. "I guess I'm in deep."

Easton

Maya downed her slushie much faster than I thought she would. We were still in line for the High Roller when I heard her straw go hollow, and though she was pleasantly buzzed by that point, I was still afraid she'd bail before we actually boarded if I didn't keep her mouth busy.

So many ways I'd love to keep her mouth busy.

I had her hold our place in line while I grabbed us two more cocktails from a nearby bar. Maya was well and truly drunk by the time we finished the High Roller, begging me for burgers. We grabbed a couple of Double-Doubles, and I took her over to another favorite place of mine.

I've been to Vegas a few times. My youngest sister had basketball tournaments here some summers as a kid, paired with a handful of twenty-first birthdays and bachelor parties.

Holding our burgers in one hand and her hand in the other, I lead Maya through The Flamingo, to the wildlife habitat behind the casino. It's not open this late in the evening, but the back doors still provide access to a quiet, plush grassy area lit by neon lights.

We sit down on the concrete steps outside the doors, and Maya sighs, her dark skin illuminated in shadows of pink. I take her burger out of the bag and unwrap it before handing it to her. The moan she lets out as she takes her first bite has my cock jumping in my trousers.

She's an exquisite fucking moaner. I would know.

"Hey," she says between bites of food. "Remember that pact we made in college?"

"Our marriage pact?" I ask.

Fuck no, I haven't forgotten, but I wasn't going to bring it up. That would mean addressing the night we had all those years ago, and I wasn't going to mention it until she did.

"Yeah." She snorts. "I thought that was so silly. I thought there was no fucking way I'd ever end up forty and un-married. And now, look at us. In our thirties and eating burgers on the ground."

I'm not sure how those things are mutually exclusive, but I'm not about to argue with a beautifully drunk attorney.

Laughing, I gently place my hand on her thigh. I pause, wanting to ensure she's okay with the touch before I begin making circles on her skin with my fingers. She sighs again, taking another bite, but my touch seems to calm her more than anything, so I continue.

"I'm looking forward to cashing in on that pact."

She turns to me, offering a lopsided smile through a full mouth. She drops her head against my shoulder, and my body ignites at the contact. Tilting my head, I let my cheek fall atop her hair, savoring the warmth of her next to me.

"I don't want to go back to the hotel yet. I want to be stupid a little longer."

"Giving yourself a break and having a good time doesn't make you stupid, Maya." I squeeze her leg. "But whatever you want, baby. I'll take you anywhere."

She's quiet for a moment before she lifts her face toward me, espresso eyes glittering with mischief beneath the lights. "You know, I bet if we pretended we were eloping, we could convince people to give us free shit."

A laugh rumbles from deep in my raging chest. "You're a menace, Maya, baby."

"A very convincing menace." I can hear the smile in her voice.

5

Easton

♥

THE SOUND IS INSULTING— incessant as the chimes and bells bounce off my skull.

An excruciating throb pounds behind my eyes, heightened by the echoing through the room and the sunlight streaming over my closed lids.

I didn't set a fucking alarm.

I turn over in an attempt to escape the light, hearing a groan leave my mouth. A matching noise rumbles through the hotel room. A second later, the chiming stops, and I settle into the pillow under my neck, ready to drift back off when I hear a stomp, a bump, and another groan.

A thought of who could be making such noises, considering I'm traveling alone, drifts past my mind, but I'm too tired to catch it.

The footsteps get closer.

That thought comes barreling back.

Who the fuck is in my room?

I shoot up, the raging pound in my head assaulting all my senses as my stomach hurls forward and my body goes numb. I slowly open my eyes, squinting at the rays of sun filtering through the window that make me feel like they're fucking bleeding.

I rub at my face, taking a moment to compose myself before I blink around the room. There is a small table in front of me, a TV across from that. I turn my head, taking a look at the bent up throw pillow wedged into the armrest.

Why was I sleeping on the couch? My room doesn't even have a couch.

Oh, fuck. "This isn't my room."

"No, dumbass. It's mine."

Even when she's insulting me, her voice sounds so pretty, I can't complain. I lift my head toward the sound of her familiar, alluring voice, watching her appear in the doorway of what I assume leads to the bedroom of the suit.

She looks almost exactly as she did last night, only a small smudge of makeup beneath each eye, the curls at the ends of her long braids a little messier. She leans against the door, rubbing beneath her eyes. A sleeveless, fitted, embroidered white dress drapes her body, hugging her curves and stopping just above the knee. A flower design accents the fabric, and she's barefoot, whereas last night, she had on those sexy as fuck pink heels.

Actually, I'm pretty sure she wasn't wearing that outfit last night.

"What the fuck happened?"

She shakes her head, turning her neck side to side, as if stretching it. "I don't remember much after the Vanderpump Cocktail Garden." She sighs. "That is, until we got back here and you kept demanding to walk me to my room. Once we got here, I didn't want to send you back alone, the mess that you were, so I made you sleep on the couch."

"Why are you wearing that dress? What happened to what you wore last night?" I ask, nodding toward her outfit as my mind reels, attempting to remember any aspect of the night.

I blank around the same time she does. I know after we finished our burgers at the Flamingo, we walked over to Caesar's and got drinks at that Van-whatever-the-fuck-she-said restaurant. I guess the owner stars in one of her favorite reality shows. We tested her theory and began telling people around the bar we'd eloped in Vegas last night, and from there, the free cocktails never stopped flowing.

"I think I might've bought this to make the bit more convincing." She laughs to herself. "I found my other outfit in a Valentino bag beside my bed."

My eyes all but bug out of my goddamn head. "You walked into *Valentino* last night to buy a wedding dress for shits and giggles?"

She shrugs, running her hands down her sides. "At least it looks good, right?"

My eyes track her movements, and I can't help the way I lick my lips as her fingers linger on the lush curve of her

waist, the flare of her hip. "Yeah, no, that dress looks—"
Something on her left hand glitters in the morning light.
"What the hell is that?"

It must've caught her eye too, because she raises her
hand, waving her fingers as the *massive* fucking diamond
shimmers bright enough to cast a rainbow throughout
the room. I don't really know how big a carat is supposed
to be, but I'm damn sure that fucker is larger than one.

"It's got to be fake, right?" She laughs again. "Sure is
convincing, though." Dropping her arm, she shrugs at me.
"I'm going to go take a shower. Thanks for last night,
husband."

That title on her tongue, with the playful wink she
tosses me before turning those flawless legs and flaunt-
ing that perfect ass in the direction of the bathroom, has
my morning wood *raging.*

The woman is downright criminal.

Husband. Fuck. Why do I like the way that sounds so
much? It's so natural coming from her, like she wouldn't
mind calling me that again. It was familiar in the way it
rolled off her tongue, and for some reason, chills race
down my spine at the thought of it.

Almost like she has said it a million times before.

And the missing puzzle piece slides into place, com-
pleting the image we painted last night.

Oh. Fucking. Shit.

Frantically, I begin pulling out the pockets of my pants,
tossing throw pillows all along the floor, searching for my
phone. I find it on the coffee table next to my wallet and

keys, my debit card staring back at me like a disappointed parent.

I open the bank app, signing into my account, and...my stomach falls out my ass. There are several less zeroes in my savings account than I had last night. My brain quickly begins to fill the gaps my drunken haze left behind.

Drinks in Caesar's. She did buy that dress, but not for a bit. For a wedding. Afterward, I bought that fucking boulder. I begin to reach into the pocket of my trousers, locating a simple black tungsten ring. The one she bought for me before we stumbled down to a little chapel and fulfilled that marriage pact from all those years ago.

"Easton!" Maya's voice is damn near blood-curdling from the other room, and I can only assume she came to the same realization.

The bedroom door flies open a moment later, and we both pause. She's staring at me where I sit on the couch, twisting the ring with what I know must be a shocked expression. I lift my head to find her holding up a piece of paper with what I can only describe as wild, frantic eyes.

"What the fuck did we do?" she asks breathlessly, enunciating each word.

"Maya, baby," I say as calmly as possible. "I think we got married."

6

Maya

"WHO THE FUCK IS Arnold?" Easton asks, rubbing the scruff on his jaw as we study the marriage certificate in front of us.

Arnold was our witness, apparently.

The signature is messy enough that whatever last name he signed isn't legible, not that it matters. Neither of us know a fucking Arnold.

And next to Arnold's signature is mine, Easton's, and the minister's. Fuck.

"Why did we do this?"

"We must've thought it was a good idea at the time." Easton lets out a breathless laugh, pointing at the date on the certificate. "Look, we must've got married after midnight, because it's dated February fourteenth." He lifts his head smiling at me. "Happy Valentine's Day."

"Isn't Valentine's Day the same day we…" I trail off, pretending like I'm not sure, though I remember the date

Easton ravished me in that library thoroughly. Ten years ago to the day.

"This cannot be happening," I mutter, because if it was, that would be fucking kismet, wouldn't it? I rub a hand down my face, biting back a yawn. "There is no way that two people who are so intoxicated they won't remember their wedding the next morning can be legally bound."

"I think that's what Vegas is all about, baby." Easton places a hand on my lower back in what I know is meant to be a reassuring gesture, but I shake off the touch. I'm too overwhelmed for it right now, and while he does have an uncanny ability to settle my nerves, it won't work this time, since he's the goddamn cause of them.

"Well, as long as we don't actually file this with the county, we should be fine. We'll just...shred it and forget this ever happened."

Easton points to the fine print at the bottom of our marriage certificate. "It says that this is a keepsake copy, not an official document."

"Fuck." I should've known, based on the showgirls and poker trips on the page, but I was being hopeful Vegas is just festive about its court documents.

"I think the official certificate is with the minister. They'll probably file it today."

I turn to face Easton. Even disheveled and in last night's clothes, he looks damn good. I like the way his five o'clock shadow has grown out, the tousled mess of hair atop his head, the way that even though I know he didn't sleep well, his blue eyes sparkling when he looks at me.

This entire situation is a fucking disaster, but I'm not sure I'd want to be caught in a storm like this with anyone other than Easton Mason.

"Do you think if we caught the minister before he delivered the marriage certificate, we could intercept it and stop this thing from being made official?" I ask.

"Maybe." Easton sighs, and it almost sounds disappointed.

I glance at the watch on my wrist, noting the time. I have forty-five minutes before I'm supposed to be at my first workshop of the day. I'm not leading it, fortunately, but considering I missed last night's dinner, I can't afford to be absent from anything else.

"I've got it, Maya," Easton says, eyeing me. "You get ready, and I'll head down to the chapel. The address is here on the certificate. I'll see if I can speak to the minister and get this all cleared up."

"Thank you," I breathe, easier than I have all morning.

Easton tosses me a crooked smile, and a need surges through my being that has me raising on my toes, pressing my lips against his cheek. I think that need is gratitude.

Easton makes me feel supported, never makes me feel alone.

He grabs my hip, steading me before placing a quick kiss against my forehead.

I can't remember the last time I felt like that. I'm the oldest daughter of three, and my parents got divorced when I was only nine. Sure, my mother and father have always been present in my life, supportive and nurturing, but when they were single, they both worked full time. It meant a lot of walking my siblings to and from school, cooking them dinner at night, and helping them with their homework. It meant living out of a duffle bag for the vast majority of my childhood, switching from Mom's to Dad's every Friday, never really feeling like I had a home.

My parents are great. They did their best, and in the grand scheme of things, I have very little to complain about, but I've been hyper-independent through no choice of my own for as long as I can remember. I wouldn't trade the skill. I like being able to take care of myself and those I love. It's a comfort to know that no matter how many times I'm betrayed or disappointed, I can rely solely on myself to survive.

But fuck, it feels nice to have someone else take care of me for once, to have someone *want* to take care of me the way Easton seems to.

"I'll come find you later," he whispers into my hair before heading to the door and pausing with his grip on the handle. "Oh, and Maya? The ring is real." Tossing me a wink, he adds, "Looks real fuckin' good on you too."

7

Easton

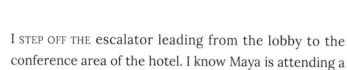

I STEP OFF THE escalator leading from the lobby to the conference area of the hotel. I know Maya is attending a number of workshops today, but I'm not sure which ones, and I forgot to ask for her phone number before I walked out of the room earlier.

My mind had been reeling.

I got married last night.

I got married, and I can't stop grinning to myself every time the thought filters through my mind. I can't stop thinking about how good it sounded when Maya called me her husband, how phenomenal she looked with that ring on her finger—so much so, I don't regret dropping the down payment of a fucking house on it.

I know, logically, these thoughts—this excitement—are crazy. I'm a lunatic, always have been when it comes to her. There was a pit in my stomach the entire walk down to the chapel, and a twinge of relief when I was told our paperwork had already been filed, that we were legally married.

Now, there is a tornado raging inside my body, elevating all my internal organs and tossing them around because I've got to go explain to my wife that she is, in fact, my wife, even though she doesn't want to be.

And the worst part of it is, I'm not sure I can say the same. I'm not mad about it at all.

After flipping through the conference itinerary, I chose the workshop I thought Maya would most likely be attending, following the directions to the conference room. I arrive just as the workshop is finishing, and sure enough, I catch Maya walking through the double doors with two men on her heels.

They both appear to be young—fresh out of law school, I'd imagine. One is tall, lean, and boyish, the other outrageously muscular but on the shorter side. I don't like either of them standing so fucking close to my wife.

Fuck. I have to stop thinking that way.

She's not really mine, and if I allow myself to get in the habit of referring to her as such, even inside my own head, I'm going to hurt my feelings.

They follow her to the refreshment table like puppies, crowding around her as she pours herself a cup of coffee. She hasn't noticed me yet, but I see her pretty lips set into a deep frown, eyelashes fluttering with annoyance as one of them speaks to her. With her shoulders tense and body rigid, I can't tell if it's the two of them being a bother, or if it's last night's nuptials still haunting her.

I step toward the end of the table—not close enough to interrupt her conversation or crowd her space, but close enough to hear the conversation at hand, listening for the right moment to step in and steal her away.

"So, what did you have to do to get chosen to be a keynote speaker? I'd love to do that someday," one of them asks.

"Did you attend my presentation yesterday? I kind of covered it there," Maya murmurs as she shakes two sugar packets and tears them open.

"Oh. Well, no. There was another speech we wanted to attend." The other one shrugs. "There was a panel with some guys who have a lot more experience. You get it."

Maya stands straight, placing a lid on her cup, forcing a smile. "Totally."

"Bu–but..." he back tracks. "You're still very impressive, especially for a woman."

Maya's entire body pauses, moving in slow motion as she turns her head to him, brown eyes fucking blazing, yet she forces that smile wider. "Can you help me understand what you mean?"

Poor boy looks terribly confused.

"I don't..." His brows furrow, and the tall man beside him looks queasy and uncomfortable. "It was a compliment."

"Oh?" Maya's voice drips with mock ignorance. "How so?"

"I said you were impressive." His tone is defensive now, and the friend beside him runs a hand through his hair, eyes darting back and forth between them, as if he can't decide whether to interrupt.

"'Especially for a woman.' I believe those were your exact words. I'm just confused by that." There is innocence in her tone, not accusation. She's playing it off like she genuinely doesn't understand the man, forcing him to explain his behavior, and the guy is *scrambling*.

A smile plays at my lips; my wife looks damn good putting a boy in his place.

"Babe, I was being nice. Take the compliment." He snorts a laugh, turning to the table as he grabs himself a coffee cup.

The dismissive action sends me spiraling, and I'm suddenly reaching out to grab his shoulder, spinning him so he faces Maya again. She gasps, just realizing how close I'd been standing, her pretty eyes widening when they meet mine.

"I think what my wife was asking you to explain is why her gender would play any type of role in the level of success she's achieved." I wrap my arm around Maya's waist. "Look Mrs. Atler in the eye and explain that to her, will you?"

His nostrils flare, jaw set tight as he gives me a once-over. Sighing dramatically, he turns his attention to Maya. "Sorry. It was a slip of the tongue. I didn't mean anything by it, really."

She levels him with a cool stare. "You should take a while to think about why you feel the need to compare accomplishments of individuals in this industry by gender, or whatever other labels you place upon us, and why the accomplishments of men might be more valuable to you than those of women." She smiles softly. "Take care."

She steps out from my hold, running her soft hand down my arm as she does so, tangling her fingers with mine. My heart rate picks up as she squeezes and begins walking out of the conference room.

I let her lead me, and once we're out of earshot, she laughs. "You know, I was going to play stupid a little longer, really torture him."

"Watching you get disrespected isn't something I'm willing to tolerate."

She pauses, glancing up at me with eyes the color of cinnamon in the light. An affectionate smile graces her lips, and she responds by squeezing my palm again. She doesn't let me go as we step onto the escalator and head downstairs.

"Were you able to take care of our issue?" she asks, and I kind of hate the way she refers to it like that.

"Why don't we grab lunch and talk about it?"

Her eyes narrow. "You didn't intercept the paperwork, did you?"

"You say intercept like I'm Jason Bourne or something." I snort. She does not match my humor. "No, I'm sorry. I missed him. It's already been filed."

"Fuck," she groans, pulling her hand from mine and tossing her head back. "I'm going to have to handle this myself."

"There was nothing I could do, Maya."

"You're a lawyer, Easton. You argue. Plead your case until you obtain the desired outcome."

I think this is my desired outcome.

I only shrug. "You're a better attorney than I am."

She rolls her eyes, and we're quiet until we reach a restaurant in the lobby and grab a table. She slips into the booth across from me, and I can tell she's annoyed. I fucking hate it, so I immediately grab her hands, bringing them to the center of the table and placing mine over them.

"I know you're stressed, and that's valid, but I promise you, I'll do whatever I can to get this figured out for us. I'm here with you," I say. She swallows, eyes dropping as she nods. "And don't let the outcome ruin the experience, please. Tell me you had fun last night, Maya baby. I'm begging."

I think last night might have been the best of my life, second only to the night I fucked her.

It kills me she may not feel the same about it.

Her lashes flutter, and a small laugh escapes her as she shakes her head. "Yeah, I had fun, pretty boy. You're a good time."

I bring her hand to my mouth, brushing a kiss over her left ring finger, noticing she must've left her ring upstairs in the room. "I'll take care of it." I lift my eyes to hers. "Of you."

"Hand kisses are legally binding," she repeats what I said last night, that breathy tone from the last time I pressed my lips to her skin back in her voice.

"I know," I say before kissing her again.

8

Maya

♥

"YOU'LL NEED TO MAKE an appointment to meet the County Recorder, and she's not available today, but I can put in an order to have your marriage certificate sent by mail if you'd like."

I rub my temples in frustration. "I need the marriage certificate now so I can get it annulled before I go back to California tomorrow."

The Bar Association conference officially ended this afternoon, and I was supposed to catch a red-eye to San Diego, but since Easton wasn't able to get this resolved earlier, we both rebooked our flights and extended our hotel reservations one more night. I'd rather this marriage in Vegas stay in Vegas.

"Well," the front desk associate tsks, "the process to annul is a bit more complicated."

"If we were so intoxicated that we didn't realize we were married until we woke up this morning and found this," I wave our souvenir copy in front of her, "I'd say that meets the criteria for an annulment."

She looks entirely unsurprised. "She has an appointment available tomorrow at ten o'clock. If you feel you have grounds for an annulment, you can obtain the proper paperwork then."

I turn to Easton, wondering if he can read the raging annoyance on my face. The sorry smile he offers me says he does, and he might be biting back an I *told you so*, because I'm having just as difficult of a time getting our godforsaken marriage certificate as he did.

"My flight doesn't leave until two tomorrow, so I can come get the paperwork," he says.

"I don't leave until four." I turn back to the worker. "Put us down for ten, then."

Late afternoon sun blasts my face as I push through the doors leading out of the dark lobby of the Clerk's office and into downtown Vegas.

"Well, what do you want to do tonight?" Easton asks as we scurry down the steps and toward the waiting cab by the curb.

"Sleep," I mutter. He opens the door for me wordlessly, and I slide into the seat before he rounds the car to the other door.

"Have dinner with me," he says as he shuffles in next to me.

"I don't trust your judgment when it comes to operating in public anymore," I murmur.

"We're already married, Maya baby. It's not like we could make things worse."

"I could get pregnant." The words leave my mouth before I've fully processed them, realizing the actual implication of my suggestion. My jaw clamps shut, and I feel warmth running up my neck and flushing my cheeks.

I glance at Easton, who has his bottom lip between his teeth, grinning with hooded eyes as he looks me up and down like he'd devour me whole in the back of this cab if I let him.

Sensation rushes south, settling in places that shouldn't be on such high alert in this proximity to him. I shove against his shoulder with mine, hiding a smile of my own as I turn to stare out the window.

When we're dropped off in front of our hotel, Easton opens my door, grasping my hand as he helps me out of my seat. He doesn't let go as he leads us through the lobby and to the elevators.

"Have dinner with me tonight, please. No alcohol. No shenanigans. Just dinner." He smiles, looping the curl at the base of one of my braids through his finger.

"Fine," I relent as we ascend, coming to a stop at his floor.

He squeezes my hand one more time before leaning in, breath warm against my ear, whispering, "And I want to see my ring on your fucking finger." His words send chills racing across my flesh, warmth gathering in my core. "Those pink heels too. I'll pick you up in an hour."

He steps off the elevator, leaving me speechless as the doors shut and I begin to ascend once more.

"What the hell is this?" I ask as we walk through a set of double doors into a poorly lit restaurant with roaring noise. Children's arcade games, I realize. "I know you don't like dark, loud, enclosed spaces," Easton says, holding onto my hand. "But I think this could be fun. This place is known for having phenomenal appetizers, so we're going to order one of each and choose our favorites, and then we're going to have an air hockey competition." He squeezes my palm. "But if it's too much, we can go somewhere else."

I squeeze back. "I can't remember the last time I played arcade games."

He glances down at me, offering a lopsided smile. "I figured."

And Easton didn't exaggerate. When we sat down at our table, he ordered us both a Shirley Temple and asked the waitress for one of everything on the appetizer menu. She had to move us from a bar top table to a booth to make enough space for the dozen plates that sit in front of us now. I'm stuffed to the brim, mostly with fried cheese.

Easton yawns, stretching his broad arms above his head, his tee riding up just enough to give me a glimpse of his stomach. I never got to see him shirtless all those years ago, and I feel it was a disservice to the experience. I'd like to see him fully, touch him—taste him—everywhere.

"You ready, Maya baby?" he asks, breaking me from my erotic, intrusive thoughts.

You have no place thinking about your husband that way.

But fuck, he is beautiful. He has a gruff exterior, tall, toned muscles that come from an active lifestyle but not necessarily a gym membership. I know Easton grew up surfing in the small Oregon town where he was raised. He snowboarded extensively through college and loved to hike on the weekends. He'd invited me numerous times, but I never took him up on the offer. His jaw is covered in a short beard—he always grew it out the same way, and sometimes, I swear, I can still remember the way it felt against my inner thighs. His thin lips are still pillow-like in softness against my skin, a contradiction to the roughness of his other features. Just like his eyes. They radiate kindness and care, even when he tries to hide it.

His hands are no different, and I watch them now as he lowers them to the table, reaching for the check. Thick veins run up the backs of them, his fingers long and wide. I've always had a thing for a man's hands. I think you can tell a lot about someone by their hands. Their size, their roughness, their cleanliness—Easton Mason's hands tell me they know exactly how to handle a woman.

"I'm going to fucking destroy you tonight, Maya baby."

I'm still staring at his hands when those words echo right through my core, lighting sparks and setting fire inside me. I inhale swiftly, loud enough for him to pause, eyes bugging as he replays the words in his mind.

"I meant at air hockey."

Unfortunately, I know.

I swallow, feeling my entire body flush with heat. Tension and time hang heavily between us, and I watch Easton's eyes dilate as he studies the reaction in my body. I lick my lips while he bites his, nostrils flaring like he can sense the arousal pooling between my thighs.

"I think...maybe..."

"You want to go back now?"

I nod furiously.

"Yeah," he agrees breathlessly. "Works for me." He slips cash into the booklet before setting it on the edge of the table, standing and reaching a hand out. "Let's get going, wifey."

I slip my palm into his as he leads me out of the arcade and through the casino until we're back on the Strip. It's not quite dark yet, but the sun has set low enough that the lights of Vegas twinkle against the orange and pink shades of the sky above our heads, casting the world around us in a plethora of color.

Easton doesn't let go of my hand as we stroll past the Bellagio fountains. Groups of people are beginning to congregate in front of them. I glance down at our joined fingers, liking the way they look together. The ring I know must've cost him a fortune blinks brightly back at me.

"We need to return these," I say, nodding down at mine and then to where the one he wears rests on his left hand. I checked my bank statements earlier today, and I know damn well his didn't cost as much as mine did, but I imagine wearing them out all day today didn't do either of us any favors when it comes to returning them later. "Hopefully, they'll still let us."

"Is being married to me so bad?" he muses, slowing our pace to a leisurely walk.

"What do you mean?"

He pulls us into a small alcove off the sidewalk in front of the fountains, taking us away from the crowd and noise. Backing me against the wall separating us from the water, he cages me in, placing his hands on the concrete behind me. "You've been married to me for one full day. Is it the worst thing in the world?"

His eyes are soft, almost pleading. Blue pools of desperation beg for my approval. I don't know why it means so much to him, why I mean so much to him, but I'm honest when I whisper, "No, not even a little." He smiles in a way that has my heart leaping into my throat. "But this isn't real life."

Easton drops his head, nose nearly skimming mine. I watch his eyes fall shut as he murmurs against my mouth, "What if we pretended it was? Just for tonight?"

The question causes my own eyes to flutter closed, soaking in his warmth and voice and aura. I'm enveloped in all his senses, and I don't want to let it go either.

"Like an experiment?" I ask, my voice coming out hoarse, strained from the struggle of holding my reaction to him at bay.

"Sure." He laughs quietly.

The sound of it caresses my searing skin, and it's instinct to arch my back, pressing myself into him. One of his hands comes off the wall and grasps my waist as his lips tickle my cheek.

"How do we do that?"

He pulls away, smiling down at me, and I'm suddenly relocating my senses. I'd become completely unaware of the environment around us—not the cool air or the night sky or the bright lights.

"Let's say we'd gotten *real life* married and had a traditional reception." He twirls one of the long braids framing my face around his pointer finger. "What song would we have danced to?"

I snort. "I have no idea."

He leans back, reaching into his pocket and pulling out his phone. "There is a song, and the first time I heard it, every time I've listened to it since..." He opens his music app before snagging his AirPods from his pocket . "I've thought of you." He places one in his ear, handing the other to me. "So, this is what I'd dance to."

I tilt my head in curious amusement, popping the bud into my ear. The soft melody of 'Pretty Boy' by The Neighbourhood floats through the speaker, drowning out everything around us, sealing Easton and me firmly inside this bubble of easy bliss.

"I love this song." I laugh.

I thought about him the first time I'd heard it, and now, I can't help but wonder if he was doing the same thing at the same moment. If we sat on opposite sides of the country, reminiscing on what could've been—the one that got away.

There are too many coincidences between Easton and I not to believe fate played some small role in our meeting and our reconnecting, I'm not sure it'd be farfetched to believe we could've discovered this evocative melody at the same time.

I let my head drop against his warm chest, snaking my arms around his neck and clasping them behind it. With my movement, both of his hands land on my waist, gripping me tightly as he turns me from the wall, swaying in circles around our small bay as the fountains erupt behind us.

I know some other music plays in the distance, I know the water is lit in color and crowds cheer around us, but none of it exists to me. There is only Easton. I'm lost in his touch, his voice, his scent.

"Sometimes, I think we hardly know each other, but other parts of me feel as if I've known you all my life," I admit softly.

His breath tickles the top of my head as he chuckles. "All I know is I liked you a hell of a lot when I was twenty-one, and I like you even more at thirty-one." If I'm not mistaken, I feel his lips press a kiss into my hair. "I don't think it'd be a stretch to believe I could like you all my life."

"You know," I muse, "that might've been the riskiest thing I've ever done, what we did in the library."

"Until you married me."

I look up at him, laughing. "Until I married you. You make me risky."

"Sometimes, I feel like an imposter. A wanderer." Easton sighs, his eyes going distant when he looks beyond me, though his grip tightens, as if I'm anchoring him. "I'm not that passionate about what I do. It just felt like what

I *should* do. It felt like it would be easier to do this than be a doctor," he shrugs, "and for some reason, I thought those were my only two options."

"Why?"

He drops his head, offering me soft eyes. "The two most influential men in my life are a lawyer and a doctor, and I guess I've always wanted to be like them. I don't know. But I'm not passionate about it. It doesn't feel like purpose." His lips tilt upward. "But when I watch you...it does. I like your determination, your ambition. It makes me want to work harder myself." I feel his hands tensing in the fabric of my dress, like he's hanging onto me. "That's why I loved being around you in college. You were the only thing that made me care. But I think you can be wound a little tight sometimes, and I don't know..." Easton smirks, those soft eyes becoming a smolder. "I like being the person to unwind you."

"More like unravel me," I murmur.

He bites his lip in that familiar way that makes me melt, sliding his hands up my back and over my shoulders. "Well, I like unraveling you."

"I still like your hands," I breathe as he brings them to my face, cupping my cheeks and tilting my head toward his.

The music still flows through our ears, though it feels more like the song runs through both of our chests, the thrumming of each chord a tether binding us together.

Easton's gaze bounces between my lips and my eyes, searching for permission. Throwing all my cautious na-ture into the breeze that is the man standing in front of me, I tangle my fingers in the hair behind his head and pull his mouth to mine.

A surprised groan escapes him, and he opens for me, allowing my tongue to slip into his mouth and dance with his. He tightens his hold on me, forcing my back to arch and our bodies together. There's no space between us, and yet, I desperately want to be closer.

It's a hunger I've never felt with anyone else, something dormant for years, suddenly reawakened by his touch. I don't know how to make sense of it, and at this moment, I don't think I want to. As Easton's mouth moves against mine and he lifts my feet off the ground, hoisting me into his arms, his hands on my hips, I feel *everything*. I'm hyper-aware of where his skin meets mine, of the way he tastes, and the pounding of my heart where it presses against his. All I want is more of it, more sensation and feeling. I want to be lost in his hands and tied up in his body, entwined with his soul.

"Easton," I breathe into his mouth. "Take me back to my room. Take me to bed."

"Yes, ma'am." The laugh he lets out against my lips is a salacious promise. "But you're getting the wife treatment tonight."

"Hmm," I muse, nipping at his skin. "You better deliver on that."

"I always do, Maya, baby."

9

Easton

MAYA'S STUMBLING, BACK PRESSED against the door as she attempts to fish the room key out of her purse. My lips are on her jaw, skating down her neck, refusing to allow an inch of space between us. Her heavy breath and soft whimpers of need tell me she doesn't mind.

Finally, I hear the click of the lock, and the door falls open behind her, both of us tumbling into her room.

From the moment the words "Take me to bed" fell from her soft, full lips, I was a goner. We raced from the Bellagio to our hotel, stealing touches and blazing through each other with searing glances. The moment I had her in the elevator alone, a decade of pining and a weekend's worth of pent up tension ripped through me. And now? I won't let her leave my sight or my arms until she forces me away.

Even if she breaks my heart with that annulment tomorrow, I'll gladly accept whatever she's willing to give me tonight—any chance to call her mine, no matter how fleeting the moment may be.

Both hands cupping her face, my lips on hers, my tongue in her mouth as I walk us across the expanse of her suite until she's pressed against the paneled windows in the bedroom that look out to the hotel's other tower across from us and the city beyond it. She feels heavenly beneath my hands, like a dream come true.

I'd spend my entire life begging for mere scraps of her attention, but having her like this? Feeling the soft sound of need float from her throat and into mine, her nails digging into my shirt to untuck it from my jeans so she can feel my skin underneath, just as fucking desperate for me? Not even my wildest imagination could conjure this. It feels as if I've hit the jackpot a million times over.

She finally works my shirt free, and her soft hands glide up my back, setting my flesh aflame as they move. She's clawing at me, frantic to get it off, and I understand the madness, because I've been waiting to see her pretty tits for fucking *years*. The last time we were together was rushed, and if this night could be our last, I won't take it for granted.

"I'm taking my fucking time with you, Maya, baby," I growl, pulling back from her.

Her hooded, brown and gold-flecked eyes appear near-black with lust as they flutter up at me, her cheeks flushed and beautiful chest heaving rapidly. Lips swollen from my kisses, body flaming from my touch, she's the most beautiful thing I've ever fucking seen.

With an immense amount of strength, I walk backward, separating us until the backs of my knees hit the bed. "I didn't get to see all of you last time, so if you want me now, I'm going to need you to show me."

First, she lifts her chin and slowly raises a brow, as if ready to challenge my demand, but something else flashes across her pretty eyes, something like unease or insecurity. "I don't look the way I did back then."

"You were perfect then, and you're perfect now," I say, softer than before. "I'm already fucking hard for you, Maya. I'm pathetically obsessed with every inch of you." I'll admit my true, deranged level of desperation if it means making her comfortable. "Do you need me to beg, baby? Because I will. Show me your body, and I'll make sure you never feel bad about it again."

I can see her attempt to fight it, but the smile my words bring to her mouth breaks through, spreading across her pretty, blushed cheeks.

"Are you ready to be a good little wife and get naked for me now?" I ask.

Biting her lip, Maya's thighs rub together, as if working to quell a burning need, a thirst only I'll be able to quench. "Yes."

"Strip."

She responds with a sultry smile, playfully toying with the straps of her dress. "Right here, in front of the window?"

I nod, settling back against the edge of the bed. "I want you backlit."

She lifts her foot, placing it against her other heel, but a shake of my head halts her. "Heels stay on. Ring stays on. Everything else comes off."

Her breath hitches, but she complies, slowly working her dress down her arms until it folds in half at her waist. She's wearing a white lace bra, and as the black dress slides down her thighs and falls to the floor, she reveals a matching pair of underwear. She kicks the garment in my direction, and I watch it soar across the room until it lands at my feet.

As I lift my eyes to her, Maya blinks innocently, removing the clip that had her hair half-up, allowing her long braids and curls to tumble down her shoulders. She's lit by blue light from the skyline behind her, casting her dark skin in a transcendent glow. She looks like the personification of temptation in her lingerie, and I am fucking desperate to be corrupted.

"I want to make you crawl."

Her lips lift, and she places her left hand on her hip, ring glittering so bright, it has my cock jumping. "I don't crawl," she says, tone pure seduction.

"Neither do I."

She leans into the glass, and through the reflection, I can see her perfect ass pressed against it, like it's fucking begging me to sink my teeth into her flesh. Raising her ring-clad hand above her head and pressing it palm down on the window, she moves at a torturously slow pace to the floor before falling to her knees.

"I don't crawl, but it doesn't mean I won't drop to my knees for you, pretty boy."

I'm fairly certain a whimper falls from my throat like a goddamn dog begging for a treat. Yeah. I was lying. I'd definitely crawl for her. Crawl, beg, bark. Sit, stay, roll over. Whatever she wants if it means my wife is falling to her knees in front of me like this. *Fuck.*

I'm lifting off the bed at what feels like the speed of light, reaching her in two long strides. Her espresso eyes are accented by long lashes as they raise to me, a picture of seduction. Dragging her hand up my jeans, she stops at the bulge behind my zipper, fingers resting over my belt buckle. "I didn't get to taste you before," she rasps. "I want to now."

Warmth erupts low in my body, spreading through my veins like wildfire and forcing itself through my throat in a groan.

"Take it out, Maya baby." The words tumble from my lips like a plea.

"Are you going to be a good husband and let me play with your cock?" Slipping my belt through the loops of my jeans, she tosses it to the floor before slowly unzipping me. "And afterward, are you going to fuck me exactly how I tell you to?"

My arm snaps out, hand gripping her chin and forcing her to lift her gaze. "I'm going to fuck you exactly how you *need* to be fucked." Dropping my hold, I growl, "Now, you be a good wife and spit on it."

Her eyes flare when she shrugs my jeans down my legs and my length springs free, swallowing thickly as she takes it in her hand. She raises her gaze to my face, our eyes locked as she leans in and spits on the head of my cock. I'm gleaming with her moisture under the harsh lights of the city as she spreads it down to my base, coating me in her.

Pausing, Maya tilts her head, studying my dick before a small, surprised gasp leaves her throat. "You're pierced."

I watch her eyes dilate as she takes in the frenulum piercing below my head. Her thumb brushes over the small, blue hoop, and sensation rages throughout my body. I hiss at the touch, and she pulls away immediately.

"It's okay. You can touch it. I like it."

She lifts her eyes. "You didn't have this before, did you?"

"No." I shake my head. "I got drunk and lost a bet a few years ago."

She huffs a laugh. "And...for women?"

"I've never had a complaint."

She hums, lifting my cock and pressing it against my abdomen before running her tongue up the back side from base to piercing, swirling her tongue around the hoop.

"Fuck, Maya," I rasp, feeling her hum against my cock at the sound. My head snaps down to find her smiling. I grip my length, outlining her lips with my pre-cum. "You look so fucking pretty like this." Her lashes flutter at the words. "Now, open that mouth. Let's see how far you can take me."

Her wet lips pop open, and I slide my cock between them until I hit resistance at the back of her throat. She gags, adjusting herself before taking me a few inches deeper, her entire mouth tightening around me. She begins to move her head, and pleasure zips down my body, gathering at the base of my spine.

My head spins, eyes rolling back, knees buckling as she hollows her cheeks, sucking deep and swirling her tongue around my cock—somehow all at the same time. Maya has always been ambitious, aiming to be the best at everything she does. I should've known she'd be no different when it came to sucking cock. A fucking go-getter, my wife is. Bet she has a praise kink too.

I'm the luckiest goddamn man alive.

Putting my theory to the test, I choke out, "Maya, baby, you're so fucking good at that. Look at you, taking my cock so deep in your throat." She moans, adding a hand to my base and moving faster. I feel like my entire body is lifting off the fucking ground. "Oh, just like that, baby. Let me see those beautiful brown eyes."

She doesn't slow her rhythm, lifting her gaze to lock on mine. It burns through me, and more than anything in this moment, it's the eye contact that sends me spiraling. I fall forward, pressing my palms against the glass to hold myself up.

I'm crowding over her, and she looks so small below me—on her knees, my cock down her throat, soft skin casted in a blue glow, braids swaying down her back. She's still looking at me, and it feels like I'm falling through her eyes, right into the depths of ecstasy.

"I'm going to come. You're too good at this." She hums, eyes fluttering at the praise, and I know I was right about that kink of hers. "I need to get inside you."

She pulls me out of her mouth, nodding fiercely. I grasp both of her hands, helping her stand before pressing her against the window and caging her in between my arms.

"Do you know what's been torturing me for ten years, Maya, baby?" I whisper against the shell of her ear before dragging my lips down her jaw.

"No," she breathes. "But what's torturing me right now is that you're still wearing a shirt."

I laugh against her neck before pulling back and lifting my tee over my head as I step out of my jeans and toss both beside us. I nod toward her chest. "Now, it's your turn. I've been dreaming about those tits for years, kicking myself for not making sure I saw them that night." I reach out and flick the strap of her bra down her arm. "What they look like." I repeat the motion on her other side. "How they feel hardening beneath my hand." I grab the cups, pulling them down to bare her chest. "How they taste."

Maya moans, tossing her head against the glass. It causes her back to arch, pressing her breasts together like they're a fucking offering. Full and teardrop shaped, they're begging for me to hold them, touch them, taste them. Her deep brown nipples are hard for me, moving with the heaving of her chest. She reaches behind her, unclasping her bra and letting it fall to her feet.

I dip my head, dragging my lips across her flesh, savoring as I move over her breast. I slip one of her nipples into my mouth, teasing it with my teeth and tongue. Her hand twists itself in my hair, tugging at its strands with her long, red nails. I suck hard before pulling away and moving to her other nipple, and Maya writhes beneath me.

"Easton, you need to fuck me now."

I groan at her insistence, the confirmation that she's as needy for me as I am for her. Quicker than she can comprehend, I pull back, grabbing her arm and spinning her so she's facing the window. I press my body into hers, watching the reflection as her tits spread across the glass.

I'm looking at Maya's face in the window as her eyes go wide—not with lust or passion, but with shock. Her palms land on the glass, a gasp leaving her throat as she whispers, "Easton, people are watching us."

My eyes snap up, and for the first time, I realize a group of four men stand in a room across from ours, peering out of its window with mirrored features of shock, if not a little hunger, on their faces. The hotel we're staying in is composed of two towers that join at their corners, forming an L shape. Rooms closest to the center sit kitty-corner to each other, with a partial view of the Strip and the other tower. Suites like Maya's have only about twenty yards of separation from matching suites on the other side, offering a perfect, clear view through one another's windows.

Maya wiggles against me, but I hold her steady. "They seem to like watching you." Keeping my eyes on the other window and the four men, I lean into Maya's ear. "Do you like it too? Do you think they might want a show?"

"Easton." She sighs, body stilling. "I... We can't."

"It's not about can or can't, Maya baby. It's about what you *want*."

"I..."

Four pairs of eyes study my wife where her body presses against the glass window thirty-two stories in the air, the lights of the city illuminating her flawless skin, naked save for the sinful scrap of white lace over her pussy and those bright pink heels that beg me to fuck her. One of them tilts his head while another adjusts himself. They look to the tallest of them, a man standing on the end of the group. I assume it may be a bachelor party, and he's the groom.

He bites his lip, but when he turns his head, his eyes lock on mine, not his friends'. Offering a shallow nod, he confirms they do, in fact, want to see me fuck my wife against this window, and God help me, the thought of doing so makes me deliriously hard.

"Do you see that, baby? They want to watch." I press myself into her, letting her feel my raging cock, and she inhales swiftly at the touch. "Does that make you wet? Knowing that when they fuck themselves tonight, they're going to be imagining you? Imagining *us*?"

"Yes." The word falls from her lip so softly, it's hardly audible. It's a truth she doesn't want to admit herself, but she's as turned on as I am right now.

"Can you show them how well you take me? How pretty you look when you're getting fucked by your husband? You do it so well, baby. You deserve to be admired for it."

"Fuck," she mutters.

I slide my hands down her arms and across her back, fastening them in the band of her white panties. I wait for her whimper of approval before I tug them down her legs, lifting her ankles to help her step out of them.

I press my lips against her shin. "I'm going to grab a condom."

"Wait," she breathes, placing a hand on my shoulder. Looking down at me, her eyes are soft and hazed. "I'm on birth control, and...I can trust you, can't I?"

I nod immediately. "Yeah, baby. You can trust me."

If I had any reason to believe I was putting her at risk, I'd grab a condom right now, but I don't, and I know if she thought the same, she'd say so.

Maya's lust-laced gaze sparkles in the low light, and her hand snaps out, wrapping her delicate fingers around my throat, tightening as she hauls me to stand. With her grip still fastened on my neck, she pulls me into a searing kiss. Her tongue dancing in my mouth, teeth nipping at my lips, I'm moaning as she whispers, "Then be a good boy and fuck me raw."

That moan morphs to a rough laugh as I grip her wrist at my throat, pulling her away and bending her arm backward before grabbing her other arm and doing the same. With them crossed behind her back, I press her against the window, noticing our audience still watching with rapt focus.

"Don't be mistaken, Maya, baby. You can own me every other second of the day..." I tug on her arms, forcing her back to arch as I grip my length. Her ass is out and perfectly positioned to take my cock when I guide it toward her entrance, both us gasping as I feed myself to her inch by inch. "But when I'm inside you, I'm in charge."

Her head lolls to the side, challenge sparking in her brown eyes. "You're going to need to earn the right to say that to me, pretty boy."

I tighten my hold on her arms, bowing her body backward as I bury myself inside her. Her breath hitches. "My God. That piercing." The word is a breathless moan.

"I know, baby. You just take it, okay?" I rocket my hips upward, watching her reflection as I hit the right spot and her eyes roll back. "Atta girl."

She cries out as I begin a punishing pace, pumping into her hard and retreating fast before repeating the motion. I watch through the glass in front of us, her pretty tits slamming against the window, her mouth opened wide and eyes blazing in ecstasy.

I look across the hotel, finding the four men still watching us. They've all taken up seats on a couch facing the window, each of them wearing an expression of equal parts envy and allure. I notice one of them as he slides his hand down his thigh, covering his cock with his palm.

"Look at them, baby girl. Look at them watching you get fucked right now." I nod toward the man touching himself. "He can't even help it. He's so hard for you." I lean into her, licking up the bead of sweat trailing down her neck. "Do you think he wishes he was me?"

She responds with a moan, moving her hips to meet my thrusts. Her pussy grips my cock like a goddamn glove, tightening with each word that leaves my mouth. She's addicted to my words, my praise, my filth. It's like she was made for me.

"I think they do," I continue, gritting through clenched teeth as she squeezes me again. "I think they'd all kill for a chance to get inside this perfect little cunt of yours." Placing my hand on the glass beside her head, I align our bodies closer until there is no part of us that isn't entwined. "But they can't have you, can they?"

"No," she whimpers, legs quivering as her nails dig into my hand where I hold her wrists in place. "They can look," she pants, breath fogging the glass, "but they can't touch."

"And why is that?" I breathe against her shoulder before sinking my teeth into her skin.

She moans. "Because I'm yours."

"That's right, baby." I drag my lips across her flesh. "Mine to touch." I deliver a swift smack to her ass with my free hand. "Mine to fuck." I enunciate the words with each slam of my cock inside her. "My." Thrust. "Fucking." Thrust. "Wife."

"Easton," she cries, her entire body trembling as she begins to go weak. I shove my leg between her thighs, holding her up. "I'm going to—"

"No, no, Maya baby." In a flash of movement, I fasten my palm over her delicate neck. "They don't get to see you come. You don't belong to them." Tilting her head back so her passion-hazed eyes fall on mine, I tighten my grip on her throat. "You look at me. I'm the one making you fall apart. I'm the man who owns this cunt."

"Oh, God," she cries, eyes screwing tight as her lips pop open and she hits her peak.

"Easton, baby. Easton," I growl, finally letting go of my hold on her arms. I keep one hand on her throat as hers fall to the glass. My other slides down her thigh, grasping beneath her knee and lifting her leg to spread her wide while I fuck her through her orgasm.

"Easton." She's shaking, crying, body vibrating as I hold her in place, never slowing my rhythm as I chase my own release. "I want you to come inside me."

Her pussy pulsates as she says the words, like she's begging me to fill it. The request has every muscle and tendon in my body going taut all at once. My vision tunnels, stars exploding in my periphery as that building pressure in my spine explodes in red hot, all-consuming pleasure.

The world warps around me, and I'm only vaguely aware of my surroundings, still entirely wrapped in the woman in front of me, in the smell of her hair and the taste of her skin, the way she takes my cock so perfectly—every goddamn inch of it. I'm pulsing, spilling myself deep inside her, and it feels like an eternity before I'm coming down from that high.

"Fuck, Maya," I breathe, letting go of her neck as we both fall against the window, entirely spent. "You are the most..." I kiss my way down her back. "Incredible—"

"They're still watching," she whispers.

My head lifts, having forgotten entirely about our audience in those final moments, too lost in the ecstasy of being inside her to know or care if our joining was being witnessed. Sure enough, all four of the men are sitting on that couch across the way, looking right through our window.

I toss them a smile, raising my hand to my head and offering a salute before I grab the wand attached to the curtains beside me, wrapping my other arm around Maya's waist and pulling her backward as I whip them shut.

She lets out a sigh as the room becomes cast in darkness. "I can't believe we did that."

"My little exhibitionist," I muse, smiling against her neck.

"Oh my God," she mutters, face falling into her hands. "That was so embarrassing."

"No, baby." I kiss her shoulder, walking us backward to the bed and urging Maya to sit at the edge. "They wanted to watch you just as badly as you wanted to be watched. You'll never see them again, and they got a far better show than anything else they would've seen in Vegas tonight."

She laughs, shaking her head, but I note the smile she's hiding behind her hands. She lifts her gaze, and our eyes clash in a mix of amusement and sated passion. "You make me reckless."

"You make me feel alive," I admit quietly, more to myself than to her. "Can I clean you up?"

She glances down, leaning back on her elbows and opening her legs, revealing the mess I've made between her thighs. A fierce satisfaction rattles me at the sight of it, my cum dripping thickly from her well satisfied body.

"Oh, yeah. Can you grab a washcloth from the—"

Her words are stopped short as I fall to my knees in front of her, gripping each of her knees and spreading her wide. Her eyes blow, breath hitching as I press a kiss to her inner thigh. "That's not what I meant, Maya baby."

10

Maya

♥

"THAT'S NOT WHAT I meant, Maya baby."

Easton's blue-eyed gaze is locked on mine where he stares up from between my thighs, on his knees in front of me. Breath is spiraling from between my lips like an F1 is raging in my lungs, because *fuck*.

He wants to go down on me right now? After he just came inside me?

I've never dated any man who was particularly enthusiastic about giving oral in general, let alone after they found their own orgasm. Most of the time, this was the point in the night when they'd turn over and fall asleep, happy to pretend I no longer existed.

"Um... Are you sure?" I ask.

"I don't think you understand what the sight of my cum dripping from your pussy does to me, Maya. I don't think you understand how fucking desperate I am to know what we taste like mixed together, because if you did, you wouldn't be asking me such a ridiculous question right now."

"Oh." The word leaves my lips a breathless gasp. I don't know how else to respond. I've never had a man react to me this way before. I don't know how to comprehend it.

"Can I eat your pussy or not, baby?" Easton's gaze rapidly darts between my face and my parted legs, damn near panting.

His reaction has me spiraling, a desperate, "Yes," falling from my lips.

A groan leaves his throat as he spreads my thighs wider. My back arches, body bowing off the bed as I feel his tongue dip into my center, the sensation heightening every molecule in my body.

He drags up my slit, settling over my clit before wrapping his lips around it. He sucks it into his mouth, eliciting sparks low in my belly, flames raging across my flesh. My hands find his hair, tangling through his chestnut brown strands as my hips move against his face, desperate for friction.

"God, Maya," he moans against me, the vibration causing my toes to curl in my heels. "You taste so good when you're full of my cum."

My head falls back against the sheets, a moan crawling out of my mouth at the feel of his words vibrating against my most sensitive place.

I feel him pull back before he says, "Do you want to taste?"

I nod frantically, and I don't know why. I never thought this would be something I was into, but somehow, with Easton, I want nothing more.

I feel him move down, dipping into my center and lapping the release inside me again. My body tightens around his tongue, desperate for more, but he leaves me feeling empty when he removes himself from between my legs and towers over the bed.

I open my eyes, finding Easton's arms pressed on either side of my head, his beautiful face hovering above me. He shifts his weight to one arm, using his free hand to grip my chin and open my mouth. "Tongue out," he demands, words muffled with his mouth full.

I obey, and he mirrors my expression by slipping his tongue between his lips. A thick, white rope of cum drips from his mouth, falling into mine. A heady mix of sweet and salt coats my taste buds as I swallow both our releases.

"What do you think we taste like?" he asks.

"Like two things that shouldn't go together but do," I breathe.

His hard expression softens, a near imperceptible up tilt of his lips. "I think we taste perfect together." He kisses me quickly. "Now, I'm going to devour this pretty pussy of ours, and I want you to ride my face so hard, those heels leave marks in my back. Understood?"

"Yes, sir."

"Fuck." He bites his lip, shaking his head as he moves back down my body to his knees. "Yeah, keep calling me that one, wifey."

Without another word, he dives back between my legs with vengeance, tongue lapping at my clit like a man starved, flicking in quick, circular motions that have my body feeling like it's floating. I do exactly as he requested, holding his head against my center, grinding my hips over his tongue. My legs are bent at the knees, high in the air to give him better access, and the tips of my heels press deeply into the skin of his back.

My mind goes numb, head spinning, unable to think of anything except chasing that high, finding that cliff, and nosediving right off it into the pits of pleasure. My cries are reaching a crescendo that echoes throughout the dark room, my hands clawing at his head as he continues his relentless pursuit against my clit.

Easton's own moan against my body sends me spiraling, and when he slips two fingers into me, curling upward and pumping at the same tempo his tongue moves against my bud, I'm falling. White light engulfs my vision, and my body goes rigid, fucking soul lifting out of my chest as I'm racketed with wave after wave of endless pleasure.

My body feels frozen as my splintered mind and fractured soul attempt to locate it again, carrying me back to myself. As I float back down to Earth, my senses resurfacing, I become aware of the soft, wet feel of lips moving up my legs. When he presses a kiss to the smattering of hair at the center of my thighs, dragging his mouth up my stomach and across my breasts before reaching my face, I finally find the strength to open my eyes and find Easton's blue ones blazing back at me.

"Hi, Maya baby."

I bracket his jaw, brushing my thumb over his short beard. "Hi, pretty boy."

He smiles, dipping his head so his mouth lands against my palm, kissing it before grabbing me beneath the arms and hauling me into his. He lifts me off the bed, and my heels finally fall from my feet as I wrap my legs around his waist.

I begin to protest, "Easton, I'm too heavy—"

"Shut up."

He carries me into the bathroom, planting me on the counter before flipping on the light. Both of us squint at the sudden brightness, but I can't take my eyes off him as he moves to the shower, turning on the water.

"Oh, we don't have to—"

He turns to me, frowning. "I want to shower with you, Maya." He brushes my braids over my shoulder before taking my face between his hands. "If I only get tonight, I want to experience it all. With you. I want to wash your body, your hair."

I huff a laugh. "It's not a hair wash night."

"Okay." He nods with understanding. "Can I still wash your body?"

"This isn't like...a seductive thing for me, Easton," I say with hesitation. "I've never showered with a man before. Bathing for me is...technical. I have a *very* specific routine I don't like to deviate from, and I already did so last night, so I'm all sorts of thrown off already. Plus, I haven't shaved my armpits in an alarmingly long time."

"That sounds seductive to me. I don't know what you're talking about."

I roll my eyes, snorting a laugh. I don't know why he makes it feel so fucking easy. Every aspect of intimacy that has frightened the shit out me seems less intimidating and more enticing when Easton Mason is involved.

Slipping off the counter, I wordlessly sort through my bag until I find my pink shower cap. Pulling all my hair over one shoulder and fisting it, I open the cap and drop my braids inside before pulling it up and over my head. It cinches at my hairline, the pink, water resistant fabric hanging at my mid back before I fold it in half and fasten the cap with a button at my forehead.

Turning to face Easton, I ask, "Am I seducing you yet?"

The smile he responds with is brighter than the sunrise. "You're always seducing me." He steps toward the shower again. "We can get in now?"

I laugh. "No." Digging back into my bag, I pull out my exfoliation scrub and body wash, handing them to him. "Put those inside the shower." As he takes them from me, I turn back to the sink and grab my cleansing balm and cleanser.

"Those too?" he asks, nodding at the products in my hand.

"Nope." I set them on the counter. "First, I need to take off my makeup, wash my face. Then, I shower. After that, it's skincare, haircare, moisturizing, and brushing teeth." Easton flicks a brow, and I toss him a dead-pan expression. "I told you, my night routine isn't sexy. It's practical, and I don't sleep well when I don't complete it."

"Maya, baby," he drawls, grabbing my hips and lifting me onto the edge of the sink. We're both still completely naked as he steps between my legs, entirely unfazed by it. "First of all, every single goddamn thing about you is sexy to me." He slides his perfect hands up my sides, studying my body before lifting his gaze to my face. "Secondly, this is a marriage experiment, no? I want to see your nightly routine. I want to see every piece of who you are."

"It's vulnerable," I admit softly, my voice no more than a whisper.

"Your vulnerability is safe with me," he whispers back, lifting a hand to cup my face.

I nuzzle into the warmth of his palm, offering nothing more than a nod. He must take it as permission, because he grabs my cleansing balm, unscrewing the lid. "This first?"

"Yeah." I reach out to take it from him, but he rears back, giving me a stern expression.

He dips his finger into the container, holding a dollop out to me. "This much?"

"Yes," I giggle. "I normally spread it between my two fingers..." I hold my hands out, showing the way I like to spread the product between my pointer and middle fingers. "And then rub small circles over my skin to remove my makeup."

He nods, following my instructions before gently pressing both hands to my cheeks. He moves over my cheek bones, nose, lips, and forehead while I remind him to be careful of my eyes. He's grinning the entire time, thoughtfully focused on covering every inch of my face.

His touch is soft, warm, delicate against my flesh, like being wrapped in comfort and care.

Once he finishes, I direct him to wet a soft cloth and wipe the balm off my face before he helps me repeat the process with my cleanser. Afterward, he leads me into the shower, adjusting the temperature of the water to a near-searing heat, even though I can tell he hates it. Easton doesn't seem to even notice when he's scrubbing my exfoliator into my skin and washing it off, doing the same with my passionfruit-scented body soap.

I wash him next, and he allows me to tilt his head back, scrubbing shampoo into his soft hair. I take my time with it, massaging his scalp and savoring his presence. I've never showered with anyone before, never known it to be something romantic. Something intimate. I don't know I've ever trusted a man the way I trust Easton, and that truth tears through me in equal parts confusion and fascination. I knew him briefly in college, and I didn't know him at all as an adult, yet somehow, after two days together, I'm terrified to walk back into a life he's not a part of at all.

After we're both cleansed, Easton wraps a towel around my shoulders and another at his waist.

"I think there are robes in the closet." I nod toward the bedroom as I step onto the bath mat.

"Got it." He darts out of the bathroom, returning a moment later with a robe on a hanger, another on his body. He helps me out of my towel before standing behind me with the robe held open, assisting me as I step into it. "What's next?"

I laugh, shaking my head. "You don't need to do this whole thing with me. You can go to bed if you want."

His brows furrow, blue eyes bright with conviction. "I don't want to be doing anything else right now."

Not knowing what else to say, I only nod. "I normally do my hair next."

"Okay." He smiles, grabbing my toiletry bag and handing it to me.

"First," I say, pulling out my scalp toner, "I'm going to spray some of this at my roots and massage it in because my scalp gets dry sometimes—especially today, since I didn't take care of it last night."

Easton gently takes the small bottle from my hand. "May I?"

"Sure," I breathe.

I watch him unscrew the cap, revealing the nozzle at the tip of the bottle. He tilts it upside down and begins raising it toward the top of my head. "Like this?"

"Yeah." I nod. "Just a few drops around the root of the braids, and I normally massage over the top of my scalp, but gently."

"Turn around and tilt your head back into my chest," he says, voice gruff and focused. I listen, feeling the steady wall of his body against my back. I let my eyes fall closed as I feel him drip the toner on my scalp before his hands begin working into the roots of my hair.

He's so careful, so calm as his fingers press and massage my head. It's almost as if I can feel the tension and stress melting from my body simply with his breath and the working of his hands. I've never allowed a man to do this to me before, never had one ask. I've never had anyone care. My throat suddenly feels tight, my eyes stinging, because I don't know how the fuck I'm going to walk away from this when it's all over.

"What made you decide to do braids like this?" he asks quietly. "In college, your hair was straight."

"Yeah," I say, clearing my throat. "I guess at some point, I realized I was cosplaying who I thought I should be, not who I really am. I needed a change, and I'd always loved this style on other women. After I took the leap and tried it for myself, it was like my insides finally matched the person staring back at me in the mirror." I shrug. "That's not to say I won't try something different at some point, but the braids made me feel like I garnered the courage to actually explore who I really want to be."

Easton's hands pause at my words, and he's quiet for a moment before he firmly says, "They look beautiful on you, and I like who you really are. I think she might be my favorite person."

My eyes flash open, finding two sapphires blazing down at me. "I like who you are too," I whisper.

He smiles, and it's almost sad, before he drops his hands from my head. "Did I do it right?"

I let out a soft laugh. "Yeah. You did great, pretty boy."

"What's next?"

I step out of his chest. "I just run some oil and leave-in conditioner through my braids to prevent frizz, then I wrap them."

I grab the products from my bag and hand them to Easton, showing him how I apply each one. He has me stand in front of him again as he works on my hair. "Don't you have any kind of routine you do?"

"I mean...not really," he admits. "My brother-in-law has an intense irrational fear of skin cancer, so he forcibly made me form a habit of putting on SPF every day."

"That's smart of him." I laugh. "I didn't know one of your sisters got married."

I remember Easton talking about his two sisters often in college. One of them was only a couple of years younger while the other was still in high school at the time.

"Well, she's not yet, I guess," he muses, finishing up my hair. "But it's coming. Penelope and Carter are..." He trails off, as if struggling to find the words. I step away from him, splitting my hair into two sections and twisting them over and around each other, forming a large bun on top of my head. "They're different. Brother-in-law is the best way to describe him. That's what he might as well be at this point."

I turn to Easton, smiling. "That's sweet."

I locate the silk scarf at the bottom of my bag, pink with small hearts all over it. I thought it would be cute for Valentine's Day, though now, the sentiment feels a little silly.

"Don't make fun of me," I murmur as I slip the scarf across the base of my neck, tugging it over my bun, wrapping it around my forehead and tying it at my nape.

Turning around, I find Easton frowning. "Why would I ever make fun of you, Maya?"

I can't help the smile that springs to my cheeks. "I bought it for Valentine's Day."

His eyes snap to the top of my head, and I watch as an effortless grin takes over his face. He surges forward, his hands bracketing my hips as he lifts me back onto the counter. Easton's mouth falls on mine, lips soft and smooth. "I love it. Very fitting." He smiles into my mouth before pulling back. "Alright, what's next?" He picks at the products lined up on the counter beside me, inspecting each bottle.

"Toner." I point to the bottle of liquid and the cotton pad next to it. "Serum." I tap the dropper beside it. "Moisturizer. Then, eye cream."

He grabs the toner and begins getting to work. "Lastly, I get to finish you off with a full body rub down, yeah?"

I snort, nodding as Easton wipes the cotton pad over my face. Next, I instruct him on the proper way to apply the remainder of the products, laughing the entire time I allow him to take care of my skin. When he finally finishes, he presses a soft kiss to my nose. "You're glowing, Maya, baby."

We both brush our teeth, thankful the hotel left my suite stocked with extra toiletries, since all of Easton's are back in his own room. Once we're finished, he carries me back to the king-sized bed in the center of the room, tossing me onto it before grabbing my favorite tub of lotion from the dressing table. "Take that robe off. You don't need it anymore."

"I need to get my pajamas," I say, though I comply with his demand.

"Oh, fuck no." He laughs, scooping the lotion into his hand and rubbing his palms together. "If I'm sleeping naked tonight, so are you."

"You can go downstairs and grab your stuff," I counter.

He pauses, tilting his head. "Why would I do that when the alternative is having you naked beside me?"

I roll my eyes, laying down on my stomach and propping my head onto my arms as Easton begins to massage the moisturizer into my skin. He takes careful consideration of my back, neck, and shoulders before moving down to my ass.

"You really do have good hands," I moan as he kneads my flesh between his nimble fingers.

"You really do have a perfect ass," he responds, massaging my thighs before nipping his teeth into my flesh.

Once every inch of my body is soft and buttery smooth, Easton flips back the comforter, and we both crawl inside. He works himself across the mattress until he's beside me, inching one arm beneath my body and the other over my side, tugging my back into his chest.

"Easton, there is an entire bed for you to sprawl out on. You don't need to be on top of me."

"No can do, Maya baby. You married a stage five clinger, I'm afraid."

I roll my head back, meeting his eyes. "I don't cuddle."

"That's because you've never cuddled with me."

I sigh, settling into his warmth. Truthfully, it's not that bad. He's warm, he's solid—comforting. His breath against my back makes me feel less alone, his hands on my skin make me feel delicate, like I'm precious. I've never felt that way through the touch of another person before.

"Happy Valentine's Day," I yawn, eyes feeling heavy as the day finally blankets over me and exhaustion settles in.

"You know, my assistant taped hearts all over my office door before I left for Vegas," he chuckles into the darkness, thumb drawing those soothing circles over my thigh. "He told me it was good luck, that it'd help me get laid by Valentine's Day."

"Guess it worked," I muse.

Easton sighs softly, breath tickling my neck. "Worked so well, I not only had the best sex of my life with the most beautiful woman on the planet, but I also got to marry my longest-standing crush."

"Easton..." I breathe, not knowing how to respond, because that statement didn't feel experimental. That statement—this entire night—is all too real.

"Go to sleep, Maya baby," he whispers, planting a soft kiss against my shoulder.

11

Easton

♥

MUFFLED WHISPERS AND THE click of a door falling into place stirs me from the best sleep I've had in years. I groan, rolling over and allowing my eyes to blink open, adjusting to the daylight floating through the paneled windows lining Maya's suite.

I'm disappointed to find the rest of the bed vacant of her, my palm stretching across the mattress as if in search of her body. I lift my head, glancing around the room, smiling as I find my wife turning the corner of the suite's main area in her white robe and rolling in a cloth-covered cart. Her hair is unwound, braids swaying at her back with each step she takes. The smile on her face tells me she's well rested, just as content with last night as I feel.

"I ordered breakfast." She slides the cart in front of the bed, lifting the silver lids covering the trays of fruit, pastries, and coffee. She crawls across the mattress, looking like my personal slice of heaven, before reaching over me to grab two mugs.

She sits cross-legged beside me, handing me my cup. We eat in comfortable silence, laughing about each other's preferred way to take their coffee and butter their toast. I like jelly, she stacks peanut butter *on top* of regular butter, which I find insane.

"We probably need to get up soon if we're going to make it to the Clerk's office in time for our appointment," she says, taking another sip of her coffee. "But I thought I'd at least get you breakfast to thank you."

"Thank me?"

She nods, lowering her coffee between her knees. "Yeah. For this weekend..." She dips her head, tucking a braid behind her ear, appearing almost bashful. "It's been a long time since I've felt taken care of, and I think...I think I really needed to be reminded of that this weekend."

Then let me continue doing it, I want to beg.

Instead, I brush my thumb across her cheek. "You deserve to be reminded of that every day, Maya."

Her eyes fall closed as she nuzzles into my palm, sighing before pulling back. "I need to go get packed. You should probably do the same."

I nod, climbing out of the bed, feeling like I'll be leaving my entire chest cavity inside this room when I exit it. I shuffle back into my clothes from last night as Maya walks into the bathroom, and I can hear her rattling through her toiletry bag.

Once I have all my things, I step into the bathroom doorway, leaning against the frame. "I'll meet you in the lobby around nine-thirty, and we can get a cab to the Clerk's office?"

She pauses, her eyes going distant as she watches herself in the mirror, refusing to look at me. Dropping her gaze and lowering the makeup brush she has in her hand, she solemnly nods. It almost seems like she doesn't want to do this, and that slight hesitation in her body language has me wanting to fall to my knees and beg her not to.

I'm far too aware of how crazy that sounds, though. I know none of this makes sense, and there is no reason the two of us should remain married, but I can't help the gnawing pit in the center of my stomach, the funneling sensation in my chest *screaming* at me not to go through with it.

Something inside me makes me feel like Maya's experiencing the same thing, but neither of us have the courage to voice it. Instead, I resolve to press a kiss to the top of her head and leave the room before she has the chance to meet my gaze.

Everything feels backward and upside down and so fucking wrong as I take the elevator to my floor, pack my things, and check out of my room. Time is warped and my vision is blurred until I'm suddenly standing in the lobby, sweating and pacing and panicking as I wait for my wife to meet me so we can end our marriage.

That thought slams into my gut like a fucking fast pitch, because I realize I didn't just accidentally get married—I accidentally fell in love, and I'm about to lose her.

I hear the elevator chime, and I spin around to find Maya stepping out of it. She's wearing a pair of distressed jeans with tears in all the right places, giving me the most enticing glimpses of her smooth, dark skin. A black tee is tucked into the waist of her jeans, accented by a pair of platform, black and gold sneakers. I can't tell the brand from here, but there is no doubt to me that they're designer.

"Hi, pretty boy." She smiles, but it doesn't reach her eyes.

"Hi, Maya baby." I smile back, knowing mine doesn't either. I take her luggage from her, wheeling it behind me as we make our way to the front of the hotel. "I already got us a cab," I say once we're outside.

I wave them down, my soul demanding I not. As the car pulls in front of us, the driver gets out, opening the trunk and beckoning for me to hand him Maya's suitcase. Yet, suddenly, my feet don't move. Neither do my arms, my mouth.

My entire body is frozen, my wife staring at me like I've lost my mind as the cab driver continues to move his arms impatiently.

Forcing myself back into reality, I turn to the driver. "Can you actually give us a moment?" The man huffs before offering me a shallow nod and sliding back into the running vehicle. Facing Maya, I find her dark eyes wide with shock and confusion, though she appears just as hesitant as I am.

"I don't want to do this," I admit.

"Easton..." She shakes her head, at a loss for words, and I can't blame her. "Are you telling me you want to *stay* married?"

I take her hands in mine, brushing my thumbs over the back of knuckles. "Yes."

"We...we can't."

"Why?

She laughs in disbelief. "We don't even live in the same state. We both have jobs and...and lives."

"My job sucks," I say honestly. "My friends are surface level. I fucking hate the cold. The only reason I came back to Boise after law school was because my firm was the first to offer me a job, and I had nothing else going for me. I still don't." I squeeze her hands. "Until you. I don't want to give you up, and the life I was living before you walked into my arms two days ago seems real inconsequential now that I realize you won't be in it when I return. You've eclipsed everything I was experiencing before, and I don't want to let that go."

Her lashes flutter, and I can tell it's an attempt to hold back the emotion crawling up her throat. "So, what? You want to move to California?"

"Sure, why not?" I chuff. "I love California. I'm always looking for reasons to go down there and visit my sisters. I've just never had the courage to stay before. You make me want to find it. You make me want to start over and finally fucking *live* for something."

"What would you do for work?" she asks, beating around every bush except the one that actually matters.

"I can work for you."

"You're not barred in the state of California."

"Then I'll fetch your fucking coffee, Maya," I scoff. "I'll walk dogs or pave roads. I don't give a shit. I just want to come home to you at the end of the day."

I watch her throat work as she swallows, contemplating my admission. "Every man I've ever dated has left me because my schedule is too busy and my job is too demanding, because I'm too detached and hyper-independent, because I don't know how to be affectionate and I don't want to be needed. Most of all," she inhales sharply, dropping her gaze to the ground, "because I don't need, and I don't *want* to need anyone else."

For the first time today, I feel my lips tilt up into a genuine smile. "Maya baby. Look at me." I grip her chin, forcing her to lift her head. "I will never punish you for being exactly who you are. I like your independence and your ambition. I love it, in fact. I want you to be all the things you just said, and I'll never try and make you different." Her brows knit together, features softening as she soaks in my words. "But I also think sometimes, you need to remember who you are outside your titles. Daughter. Sister. Attorney. I think this weekend you were reminded, maybe for the first time in a long time, what it's like to just be Maya. My Maya."

One rogue tear escapes her glistening eyes, cascading down her cheek before I catch it. She nods, and I lift the hand of hers I'm still holding to my mouth, pressing my lips against it.

"I started falling in love with you ten years ago. Every study group, every stroll between classes, every stolen glance in the library, I was tumbling head first into it.

What I've realized now is that the timer didn't start over despite the years apart. No, it began ticking faster the moment I was back in your presence."

"You love me?" she asks, the question a gasp.

I know I may have said too much, laid myself too bare. I don't think anyone has ever said something like this to her before, and while a deep satisfaction runs through me knowing I'm the first, I also know it's going to take a minute for her to process. There were about a million ways I could've gone about this conversation, and the front entrance of a Vegas casino while a very impatient cab driver honks at us aggressively wasn't the place to do it.

"Give it two weeks," I plead, tone coming out shaky and desperate.

"Give what two weeks?"

"Yourself," I continue. "Give yourself two weeks to think it through. Please." I kiss her hand again before rolling her luggage in front of her and grabbing mine. "I have a trip planned to see my sister at the end of the month in Los Angeles. I'm going to go grab the annulment papers right now, and I'll bring them to you then. I'll have them signed, and if you still don't want to give us a shot, we'll file."

"Easton..." She sighs. "I...." Her eyes are frantic with confusion and unease, but she's not telling me no.

"Please." I lean forward and kiss her head. "Please, Maya. Just...think it through." I grab my bag and toss it in the back seat of the cab before stepping one leg in. "You stay, and I'll—"

"Wait!" she says, stepping off the curb. "Our rings. We need to return them."

The removal of that ring from her left ring finger is like a hot blade slicing itself down the center of my heart, and I swear, I can almost feel both halves of it splatter against the concrete beneath my feet. She holds it out to me, and the expression on her face is unreadable, the only sign she's feeling any emotion at all the tear slipping down her cheek.

She extends her hand to me, holding out the ring, and I'm obliterated as I take it from her. I slip mine off too, and she opens her palm. I place both inside it, curling her fingers over top. "I understand you need to return my ring, but this one is always going to belong to you. I won't take it." I kiss her knuckles. "I will come find you in two weeks, I promise."

She blinks down at the two sparkling pieces of jewelry she's holding, and before she can say anything else, I fall into the back seat of the cab and shut the door. The driver pulls away, and I'm too terrified to face whatever expression she may be providing me. I let my head fall into my hands, refusing to look back as we drive away, leaving my shattered heart right at her feet.

12

Easton

Two Weeks Later

DISTRICT COURT, CLARK COUNTY, NEVADA stares up at me menacingly from beside my desktop. I'd been told an annulment for Maya and I would be incredibly easy to file, considering we didn't live in the same state and had virtually zero ties to each other outside the attendance at the same conference and a degree from the same pre-law program.

That felt like another punch to the chest.

I signed the papers when I got home from Vegas and have kept them beside my desk, an aggressive reminder of the complete ass I made of myself in front of the hotel two weeks ago.

Once the adrenaline wore off, I realized what a ridiculous request I'd made of her. It wasn't plausible for me to think Maya and I could just...stay married. To think that she'd even want to—she has an incredible career, her family, probably friends too. Fuck, I don't even know if she has friends or who they are.

None of it makes sense—my feelings, this marriage, my rash decision to leave Maya standing on that curb as I drove away. I feel ridiculous, but I can't take it back, and I'm not even sure I want to. Regardless of how crazy I looked and how desperate I sounded, every word that spilled from my mouth that morning was true and real. At the very least, Maya deserved to know.

I suppose it's not a bad sign that she hasn't contacted me either. She easily could've obtained the paperwork herself and had me served. She hasn't, and I've had no contact with her, which must be something, right?

My insides twist and knot themselves together as I tap my hands on the top of my desk, watching the clock. I have approximately four hours before I need to catch my flight to LAX. I'll stay with Penelope and Carter tonight before heading down to San Diego tomorrow. That's when I'll face Maya and quite probably go crying home to my baby sister, Maddie, after my wife leaves my heart in pieces.

There is a soft knock outside my office door before Derrick peeks his head inside. Concern is present on his face, but it's nothing new. I've been a complete downer since I returned from Vegas, and as much as I do actually like the guy, I'm in no place to explain myself to him.

"You have a visitor," he says quietly.

"I'm not taking any more meetings today," I mutter, avoiding eye contact as I click across my screen.

"Um...I think you'll want to take this one."

I lift my eyes, finding him swiveling his head to the door, as if he's looking at whoever is asking to meet with me. I hear a muffled mutter and watch Derrick's eyes go wide before he's stepping aside. The door swings open completely as my wife barrels through it.

Maya

Easton's mouth drops open like he has seen a ghost, rolling back in his desk chair like he can't figure out if I'm real or not.

I turn to his assistant, smiling sweetly as I grab the handle. "Thanks so much, Derrick. I'll take it from here."

The boy cocks his head, not making any movement until the door is nearly hitting him in the face, and he jumps back just as it clicks shut. I spin, walking right up to Easton's desk in the corner of the office and sliding myself to sit atop it. "Hi, pretty boy."

"Maya, baby." His face is pale, eyes fearful, and I hate that he's feeling that way. "I have a flight booked to Los Angeles tonight, I swear. I was going to come see you tomorrow."

"I know." I nod. "But I came to you first."

"Why?"

"Because..." I swallow my nerves. "You made your grand gesture, and it's my turn to make mine." I feel my bottom lip begin to tremble as my voice cracks on the words. "You told me you loved me."

"Love, not loved." His chest is heaving, features frantic, like he's hanging onto every sentence leaving my mouth.

I nod. "It's my turn to do the same."

Easton's lips part, quick breath escaping them in rapid bursts as his brows knit together.

"There are certain things about me that people feel compelled to change. My family. The men I date. I need you to understand that I do not want to change, and I won't be with someone who tries to force it upon me." I turn my legs, angling myself toward him, and our knees brush. "I'm never going to believe anyone else can take care of me as well as I take care of myself. Sometimes, I'm not the most thoughtful person. I forget birthdays and anniversaries. It's not on purpose, but it happens, even when I try my best. I'm not a great gift giver, and I don't think I'm very good at showing my love, but it doesn't mean it doesn't exist. When I'm overwhelmed, overstimulated, and overstressed, I self-isolate. I don't want to be coddled or suffocated. I don't like to cuddle..." I smile creeps up to the corner of my mouth. "I mean...I did like cuddling with you, but I don't know if I'll want to every single night."

Easton's hand softly finds itself on my thigh, rubbing those comfortable, soft circles with his thumb.

"My self-worth is always going to be led by my accomplishments, and because of that, my ambition will never be satisfied. I love my job. I love helping my authors make their dreams come true, so I work nights and weekends and holidays. I travel a lot. I put my career first, and as unhealthy as it may be, I likely won't ever stop. It's what gives me contentment, but..." I sigh, placing my hand over his. "This weekend, I realized it doesn't have to be the only thing giving me contentment. I think you might do that too." I lift my eyes from our joined hands to meet his face. "For the first time in my life, I want to be dedicated to something outside my work. I...I want to be dedicated to you, Easton. I want you to be dedicated to me." A lump works its way out of my throat, showcasing my choked emotion. "I want you to be dedicated to exactly who I am at this moment—not who I was ten years ago, and not someone you hope I could someday be. I need to be loved for being just me, and if you can't do that, then—"

He cuts off my words by surging forward, sealing his lips to mine. Cupping my face and forcing us closer, he kisses me with enough intensity to set my chest aflame. He kisses me like he has waited his whole life for it, like whatever has erupted between us is finally real. Easton kisses me like a promise, like I'm something to cherish, no expectations and no conditions.

"I love exactly who you are at this moment, Maya. I love who you were ten years ago, and I love every version of you you'll become. I know you, and I may not remember doing so, but I know what I signed up for when I signed that paper, and I think it's the best decision I've ever made." He kisses me again. "Now, can you tell me you love me back?"

I smile, running a hand through his soft hair. "I love you, pretty boy. I love you for exactly who you are, for all the ways you drive me mad and make me laugh. I love you when you think you don't deserve it, and I'll do my best to show you that you do."

He drops his head, our nose and lips and hearts aligning. "I don't know who the best version of myself is yet, but with you, I think I'm finally ready to figure it out."

"How are we going to do this?" I ask, brushing my thumb across his jaw as he brushes his lips against my nose.

"I'm going to hand in my resignation. We're going to California tonight so you can meet my sisters. Then, you're going to show me where you live, where you work. I'll apply for a job, you'll interview me, and even though you'll play hard to get, we both know you're gonna make me an offer." He smiles against my lips. "Then, I'll sell my condo here and move in with you, or we'll find a new place together."

"I'm not moving, I love my apartment." I giggle into his mouth. "Though, you should know, I've already taken up both the His and Her closet spaces, so you'll have to use the guest room."

He laughs, nodding. "I think I can agree to those terms."

Pulling away, he takes my hand, helping me off his desk. I watch him open a drawer, taking out a laminated folder with one sheet of paper inside. Next, he dumps his laptop and nameplate into his briefcase before tugging me out of the office with him.

We stop in front of a door at the end of the hall, and he knocks once before walking inside. An older gentleman sits behind the desk, snapping, "What do you want, Mason?" without bothering to look up.

"Harvey, this is my wife, Maya Atler."

His head snaps up immediately, eyes narrowing at Easton before flashing to me. They soften as he gives me an unashamed once over, raising an impressed brow before darting back to Easton. "Are you kidding?"

He smiles, proudly grasping my left hand and raising it to his lips, my massive ring glittering in the sunlight through the window. "Nope."

The man turns his attention to me. "How'd a pretty little thing like you end up with an idiot like him?"

I hear Easton sigh beside me, his hand tightening in mine. His body language shifts, and I know the comment got to him. It makes me wonder how many remarks like this he has taken on the chin throughout his career, how often he had to pretend he's not offended while his terrible boss chipped away at his self-worth little by little.

"What do you mean by that, Harold?" I ask, turning back to Harvey.

"It's Harvey, sweetheart." He looks me up and down again, blatantly pausing on my hips and chest before biting his lip. "And I was making a joke."

Easton scoffs loudly, a wide grin spreading over his cheeks as he lets go of my hand and steps up to his boss's desk. "I quit." Leaning over it, he slides his letter of resignation in front of the man. "Now, you're going to take your eyes off my wife, and if you disrespect her one more time, I'll put you through that fucking window."

Harvey's mouth drops open in shock, his head swiveling to me as if I'm going to condemn Easton's behavior. Instead, I toss him a sickly-sweet smile. "And if you ever insult my husband's intelligence again, I'll do the same."

Easton stands, straightening his tie before grabbing my hand and heading to the door. "I'll have Derrick clear out my office before the end of the day, and I'll coordinate a time to grab my things with him directly. Good fucking luck, Harv."

We exit his office without another word, leaving him gaping like a fish.

As the elevator door shuts in front of us and we descend to the ground level of the building, I say, "I think we should ruin his life."

My husband chuckles, bringing my hand to his mouth as he brushes a kiss across it. "You're so sexy when you're a menace, Maya baby."

13

Easton

♥

MY CHEEKS ACHE FROM the weight of the grin I haven't been able to let go of for the past twenty-four hours. Yesterday, after I handed in my letter of resignation, Maya and I got her added to my flight to LAX—along with a First Class upgrade she *insisted* on—and we landed in Los Angeles late last night.

Rather than having my sister pick me up from the airport as initially planned, Maya and I booked a hotel near Penelope's apartment complex—another top floor suite—and made good use of those paneled windows too.

Now, my hand is splayed over my wife's thigh, her small fingers wrapped in mine, the ring I bought her sparkling, and I have my own ring back too. As our ride pulls up in front of Muse, I watch Maya's breath pick up before she turns to me. "I'm nervous."

"Don't be." I raise her hand to my lips. "Penelope's like a tabby cat. She's only going to scratch you if it's really warranted, and if anything, she'll be more concerned for you being married to *me* than the other way around."

She tilts her head at me. "Why do you do that? Think so lowly of yourself?"

"Self-deprecation is my sense of humor, I guess?" I flash her an unconvincing smile.

Her features are serious when she responds, "You are worthy of being my husband, Easton. It's an insult to me to insinuate otherwise. I'm not an idiot, and I wouldn't marry one either."

I nod rapidly. "Sorry, baby. You're right."

I squeeze her hand before getting out of the car and rounding the other side to open her door. As she steps out, she brushes her hands down her jeans, straightening out her sweater and tugging on the bun atop her head. "Do I look okay?"

"You're perfect." I kiss her cheek before tugging her hand and leading her inside the art gallery Penelope and Carter own.

Muse is structured to feel breezy and freeing, decorated in shades of blue and beige with terracotta accents, a trickling waterfall in the corner of the entry, and soft instrumental music playing throughout the open space. One may mistake it for a day spa rather than an art gallery.

All the pieces feature local or up-and-coming artists, and everything is centered around nature and landscapes. Podiums are spread throughout the large main room with sculptures, and paintings are strung on the walls, with one corner of the gallery focused on photography.

The door chimes when it clicks shut behind us, and a soft voice calls, "I'll be right with you!" from the office behind the reception desk. I recognize my sister's musical tone immediately, smiling to myself as I walk Maya through the gallery while we wait.

Our hands are linked as we stroll through the space. She points out several paintings, and I'm fairly certain a number of them were done by my sister. Finally, I hear the stomping of feet making their way in our direction from behind me.

My sister has always been a stomper. As a kid, if she was up walking around in the middle of the night, the entire house was woken from it. That girl never got away with so much as sneaking a midnight snack from the kitchen because she's unknowingly loud as fuck.

I spin around, and my little sister is throwing herself into my open arms. Her deep red hair sways against my hands as I wrap them around her, and she locks hers at my waist. "Hi, Pep."

"Hi. I missed you," she mumbles into my chest.

"I missed you too." I squeeze her before letting go.

As she takes a step back, her massive green eyes finally fall on Maya. "Oh." She blinks. "I'm so sorry. I had tunnel vision." Penelope chuckles, holding out a hand. "Hi, I'm Penelope."

Maya returns the gesture, shaking my sister's hand. "Maya."

"Pep, Maya is my wife," I proclaim proudly.

"Oh." My sister's mouth drops open, and she freezes. Maya drops her arm, looking at me with an unsure expression as Penelope's gaze darts back and forth between the two of us rapidly. "Sorry, did you say wife?"

I open my mouth to respond, but before I can, I'm interrupted by a gruff, "You've got to be fucking kidding me."

Not a second later, my sister's boyfriend appears beside her. Carter throws an arm over Penelope's shoulder, and she finally unfreezes, body immediately relaxing.

"You got married? Like actually?" he asks, hazel eyes narrowing on me.

I grin. "Beat you to it, motherfucker." Holding up her hand, I showcase Maya's sparkling ring.

Penelope's jaw sets, and her eyes flutter with annoyance as she glares up at her boyfriend, shoving herself out of his arms. "Sorry, he is so incredibly rude." My sister opens her arms, offering Maya a hug. "I'm so happy to meet you, and I'd love to know the entire story of how this could've possibly happened."

Maya's eyes flash to mine, shining happily as she returns my sister's embrace. "I'm so happy to meet you too."

As they separate, Carter holds out his hand to Maya. "I'm not actually rude, I promise. Your husband has been harassing me for twenty years because I've been begging his sister to marry me since I was nine. I'm sure you can understand my frustrations." Maya's features glitter with amusement as she takes his hand in hers. "Congratulations. It's lovely to meet you."

"You too." She laughs before glancing at me. "Sounds like *you're* the menace."

I slip my arm around her waist, tugging her against me as my lips brush her forehead. "I've got nothing on you, Maya, baby."

"It's actually a family trait. Welcome." Carter smiles.

Penelope scoffs, rolling her eyes. "I told him I'd marry him after I got my PhD. He's just impatient."

"Sounds like you're a girl after my own heart." Maya laughs.

"Macie will be here in about fifteen minutes to watch the desk, and then we can go get lunch. You guys are more than welcome to take a look around in the meantime, or if you want to rest for a second, you can head to our apartment upstairs."

Macie is Penelope's best friend and the gallery's event coordinator. She'll sometimes manage operations when Carter is busy, and she's currently about five months pregnant with her first child. It'll be interesting to see what kind of kid she pops out, because if my sister is a tabby, Macie is a fucking bob cat, and her husband, Dominic, is just as wild as she is.

Maya crosses her arms, glancing around. "Are all the pieces here for sale? We actually just expanded some of the space in my office, and I'm still trying to decorate. I've been meaning to snag some pieces, and I love supporting local artists."

"I can show you a couple of things." Penelope smiles, taking my wife's arm. "What do you do?"

"I own a law firm, Atler and Associates, in San Diego. We specialize in publishing and literary law. Working with authors, mostly."

"That's incredible."

Their voices trail off as Penelope leads Maya through the rest of the gallery. I follow Carter over to the front desk, leaning my elbow against it as I watch them.

"She seems great, Easton. Congratulations," Carter says, clapping a hand on my back.

"I know. She is." I smile. "We got damn lucky."

My eyes flick to him, watching his smolder like embers as he looks after my sister. "Yeah, we did."

14

Maya

Valentine's Day - One Year Later

"E, BABY? I'M HOME!" I call, setting my keys on the entry table and closing the front door to the apartment behind me.

I'm immediately hit with the aroma of chicken and Italian spices. The sun is just beginning to set in front of the expansive windows lining our unit at the far side of our living area, the view overlooking the Pacific.

"In here." My husband's soft, deep voice responds, and my heels click against our tile floor as I turn the corner into our kitchen, finding Easton behind the stove.

He left the office about an hour and a half before I did. I do my best to take off with him at a reasonable time each day, but I had an author who wasn't available to meet with me until after hours from her own day job, and if my clients are up into the late night working toward their dreams, I want to do the same.

In the past, after working late, I'd typically come home to white wine and Goldfish for dinner. Now, Easton always makes sure I'm well fed, well fucked, and well cared for before my head hits the pillow at night. He never gets angry at me for opting to work late or on weekends, and if I have to travel, he accompanies me.

We continue making excellent use of every hotel room we stay in, especially the ones on my business trips to New York, San Francisco, and London. Not only is my husband great in bed, against window, and on table, but he's also phenomenal in the back seat of my car, the kitchen counter, the balcony railing, and the desk in my office—both at home and the firm. And I can't even begin to think about that stage in Amsterdam without needing to change my panties.

I sigh, tongue in cheek as I reminisce on the enticing experience, being pulled from the reverie when Easton kisses the top of my head. "How was your meeting?"

"Good." I duck into our bedroom, kicking off my shoes and tossing my dress before sliding into a pair of joggers and a hoodie. "Is that your mom's creamy chicken pasta I smell?"

"Yep! Figured I'd do something special tonight."

I return to the kitchen, pulling out a barstool across from where he's standing. He lifts a fork to my mouth, and I take a bite of the chicken smothered in cheese and herbs, moaning as I chew and swallow. "What's so special about tonight?"

He tosses me a glare, though he knows I've not forgotten. In fact, I gave him my anniversary present already when he woke up this morning with my lips around his cock.

February fourteenth is special for a whole slew of reasons, but I know tonight is going to cement that fact much more deeply.

"I haven't given you my gift yet either. Figured I'd do it over dinner," he says.

"The two orgasms this morning weren't my gift?"

He pauses, wooden spoon in hand, tossing me a dead-pan expression. "Baby, that's just part of my daily routine."

My lips ache at the force with which I'm holding back my smile, knowing I'm losing the battle with the flush creeping up my cheeks right now. Easton smirks triumphantly to himself as he plates our food and walks over to the dining room table that looks out to our balcony and the horizon beyond it.

There's a bouquet of pink and red flowers, plus a box of candy hearts that he surprised me with this morning, still sitting at the center of the table, along with my favorite wine and a plate of chocolate-covered strawberries Easton must've picked up on his way home from work. He sets our plates next to each other, and I slide into my seat.

He offers to pour my wine, but I decline, opting for water instead.

As we both dig into our food, Easton straightens his leg and reaches into his pocket. "Okay, are you ready for your gift?"

"Actually..." I say, standing from the table. "I have one for you too. Let me grab it."

I dart into the ensuite off our bedroom, sifting through the drawers on my side of the sink until I find what I'm looking for and slip it into the pocket of my hoodie.

"I didn't have time to wrap it. Sorry." I sit back down, returning to my food. "So you should close your eyes when I hand it to you."

He cocks his head, bemused. "Okay, fine. But you have to close your eyes too then."

"I can agree to those terms." I wink.

He chuckles, closing his fist around something. "Alright, you ready? Hold out your hand and close your eyes."

I nod. "You do the same."

I watch his lids fall shut just as mine do the same, and with darkness blanketing my vision, I reach into my hoodie pocket before gliding my closed fist across the table in search of his hand. While I'm doing so, I feel my left hand get flipped over, palm down, and I immediately know what my gift is as I feel it slide onto my finger.

I drop what I'm holding into Easton's outstretched palm when he says, "Okay, can we open them?"

"Yep." My stomach knots itself together, and I can feel the chicken swirling inside it, suddenly begging to come back up. I know I have no reason to be nervous. I know Easton is going to love it, but I can't ignore the small part of me that's absolutely terrified to see his reaction—mostly because I'm terrified myself, and if he acts the same, I might lose it.

I open my eyes, and they immediately fall to my left hand. Sure enough, a diamond-studded band, the perfect accent to my ring, sits just above it on my finger. Technically, Easton never bought me a wedding band, just the ring when we were in Vegas, and while we've been legally married the past year, it has felt more like dating. We live together, we work together, but we've also spent a lot of time getting to know one another and each other's families, integrating our lives in a way that works for both of us.

It has been trial and error, and hard in some moments, but we decided when the time was right, we'd renew our vows in a more traditional setting. Sure, it had been born from the insistence of both our mothers and our siblings, but we want that for ourselves too.

I figured I'd worry about getting a wedding band when we were ready to take that step, and I wonder if Easton's gift is his way of telling me he is.

I think my gift might be my way of doing the same.

"It's beautiful, E," I breathe, moving my hand in a way that allows the diamonds to reflect against the fading daylight outside our window. "I love it."

He doesn't respond, and I lift my eyes to gauge his reaction when I find him frozen, staring slack-jawed at the pregnancy test in his hand. His chest is expanding frantically with each rapid burst of breath from his parted lips, like his mind is sprinting.

"E, baby... Say something."

His eyes finally flash to mine, and that's when the building moisture welled within them spills over. His exhale is audible, a gasp of surprise before his mouth morphs into the brightest smile I've ever seen on another human being. "You're pregnant?"

"Yeah," I whisper. "Are you mad?"

His brows knit together. "Mad? Why would I be mad?"

"I don't know... It wasn't like this was entirely planned." I got off birth control a few months ago, opting to track my cycle instead. I'll admit, we weren't the most careful, mostly because for the first time in my life, I trusted someone enough that I didn't feel I needed to be. Still, we'd planned on having our vow renewal and crossing a few more international trips off our list before we had a baby.

"Fuck, Maya. I don't care." He stands abruptly, kicking his chair out behind him. Our dinners sit on the table, entirely forgotten as he slides the plates out of his way, grabbing me by the hips and setting me on our table. "This is the best day of my life. Are you kidding?"

He drops to his knees in front of me, lifting my sweat-shirt to reveal my bare skin. He places his large hands across my stomach, the tendons in his fingers working deliciously as he runs his fingers over my flesh.

"How far along?" he asks, lifting his blazing blue eyes to me.

"I don't know yet. I'm only about a week late, but you know how I feel about punctuality, so I took a test this morning. I'll call the doctor tomorrow to schedule an appointment."

He nods, planting his lips over my belly as his arms slide around my hips, pulling me into him. "Thank you," he murmurs against me. "Thank you for giving me this."

I run my fingers through his hair. He has told me a few times that he always wanted children, and as I look down at the way he tenderly handles my mid-section in his soft hands, the way he whispers his gratitude into my skin, the way his lips brush over the wet marks his tears left, I know he'll be the most excellent father.

"I'm a little scared," I admit quietly, mostly because, for all the confidence I have in him, I'm not sure I can say the same for myself.

He looks up at me, resting his chin against my stomach. "I know. It'll be scary, but we'll figure it out together. We're going to do great."

"What about our jobs? Neither of our parents live nearby, neither do my siblings, and yours are busy. We're kind of alone out here, but I don't want to leave California. I just don't know how we're going to do this without help. I don't know how to baby."

His brows furrow before he lights up with laughter. "I don't know how to baby either. But we can take classes, and last I checked, our parents have cellphones, so that's good. There are books to read, YouTube videos that'll teach you how to do anything."

I frown, because YouTube parenting advice doesn't make me feel confident in the slightest.

"I'm kidding, Maya baby. We'll be okay. I'm sure our families will fly out for the first little while until we get the hang of things. After that, we can look into getting a nanny, or find a great daycare, or...I could stay home with the baby."

"Are you serious?" I ask.

He stands, keeping his hand on my stomach. "Fuck yeah. I've always wanted to be a dad. I can't wait to coach soccer teams and carpool. Fuck it, I'll drive a minivan. I don't care."

"We will never own a minivan."

"Fine," he scoffs. "I'll settle for a Yukon then." He takes my face between his hands, resting his lips against my nose. "I can still work for the firm from home, reviewing contracts and whatnot, but while you handle the bestsellers of the world..." He smiles down at my belly. "I can be here with nugget."

"We're not calling them nugget."

"I was eating chicken when you told me. You set us up for this, Maya." He rubs his hand over me. "Hi, nugget. Daddy loves you already."

I sigh; I can't help the flutters inside me at the way he's already referring to himself as *Daddy*, the affectionate tone he's using when speaking to my stomach. There is no doubt it'll be challenging, and sometimes, I'll be afraid, but I know there is no one else I'd want to have a baby with, no one else I'd rather call my husband.

Easton Mason is it for me.

As if I'd said the words aloud, his eyes snap to mine, boring through me. Golden light filters across his face, setting him on fire. He cups my cheek, and I nuzzle into the familiar warmth of his touch.

He inches into me, feathering his lips between mine. "I love you, Maya baby."

I smile against his mouth. "I love you, pretty boy."

Acknowledgements

What a whirlwind writing this little story was! I'd never planned on giving Easton a book (in fact, I very adamantly insisted I'd never give him a story to anyone who asked), but I'm so glad that I did. This one was so much fun to write. It seems with each work I publish, the acknowledgments get longer and longer, but what a special thing that is.

I want to thank Jenna for being by my side for every win, loss, challenge, obstacle, and mental breakdown. For taking so much off my plate so that I have the ability to even consider writing a book in three weeks, and standing beside me while we pivot all of the marketing plans we spent months creating to rapid promo this story and get it in front of as many readers as possible. I also want to thank you for always keeping faith in me, especially in the moments when I don't have much belief in myself. Your role as my Brand Manager is priceless, but your role as friend means even more.

My editor, Alexa, for helping inspire this story and supporting me through my brainstorming phase as I asked you a million questions about being a lawyer. For taking on this manuscript SO last minute and making it beautiful, and for supporting and uplifting my business and journey as an author. I am endlessly grateful to have you in my corner, and I couldn't do it without you!

My sensitivity readers, Lexi and Joc. First of all, everyone should thank Lexi for relentlessly pressuring me to give Easton a book for the last year. She's been asking for this since she read The Soulmate Theory, and I'm happy I could finally deliver, you saw him for the slutty little golden retriever he always could be. I hope I did him justice. But more importantly, thank you both for helping me develop Maya's character. I've fallen so in love with her, and I'm forever grateful. Also, shoutout to Bri for reading through the hair care and your feedback on Maya's braids. I don't know if this is your first time being added to the acknowledgments of a book, but I hope it is and it excites you. You're a real one and I miss you!

My PA, Cassie, for taking so much pressure off my shoulders that allows me to spend more time with my characters and crafting stories, and for putting all of your heart and dedication into your work, from the beautiful content you create, to your enthusiasm when engaging with my community about my books. I'm so grateful I found you when I did, and that I get to have you on my team as I navigate this crazy business.

Miss Tori Ann Harris, thank you for taking a break from your regularly scheduled Leo Graham bullying to read this story early. I dread the day I write something that doesn't cause you tears.

My street team for taking the massive pivot from Reckless Roses to The Forever Experiment and just completely running with it from the last minute cover reveal to the last minute ARCs and rapid release time. You have all been endlessly supportive in the crazy changes happening and always jumping in to uplift my stories. I couldn't do it without you and I love you so much!

My Patreon girlies for supporting me on a deeper level, and always being excited to live in this crazy little universe with me. I love sharing this world, these characters and stories we love so much. You all constantly remind me what I love most about being an author, and that's connecting with others through the art of storytelling. Your support keeps me grounded when everything feels up in the air.

My Bubs. Thanks for eloping with me in Vegas so that I could relive that weekend while writing this super fun little story. Thanks for taking this hyper-independent eldest daughter and teaching her how to accept love. And most importantly, thanks for being an acts of service golden retriever who knows how to wear a leash and hold it too.

My best friends (besides those already mentioned) Emily, Ivy, and Ambar for letting me yap and cry and complain and brainstorm, for always supporting me, and for being my life vest when I feel like I'm drowning. I love you guys so much and I'm so grateful for you!

Lastly, to any and everyone who's picked up this story and made it this far. Thank you for reading and supporting my dreams. I hope you loved Maya and Easton as much as I do, and I hope you'll stay along for ride.

Also by Sarah A. Bailey

The Soulmate Theory
The Fate Philosophy

The Pacific Shores Series:
Heathen & Honeysuckle
Wicked & Wildflower

About The Author

Sarah was born in California and raised in Southern Oregon, and still considers herself to be a Pacific Northwest Gal at heart; right down to being a coffee snob, collecting hydro flasks, adamantly believing in Sasquatch, and never having owned an umbrella.

She now resides in Arizona with her husband and their pup, Rue. When she's not writing, she's likely reading, and if she's not reading, she's probably out searching for a decent cup of coffee or binging Vanderpump Rules for the millionth time.

Stay connected with Sarah by following her on social media @sarahabaileyauthor, or signing up for her newsletter: